Grand
v
Germany

JOHN MANNING

FOR MY WIFE GILLIAN

Without whose help this book would never have been written,
let alone published.

First published 1995

Made and printed in Great Britain by
The Guernsey Press Co. Ltd, Guernsey, Channel Islands

ISBN 0 9525447 09

Cover illustration by James Hall

Also published by John Manning
Parish Pump
Parish Pump 2
Glimpses of Jersey
Glimpses of Guernsey

CONTENTS

Page

1   Land of Hope and Glory 1

2   The Ahier Family 2

3   Enter the Germans 9

4   Rules and Regulations 12

5   Visitors 14

6   The V Signs 24

7   Grandpa 1 - Germany 0 30

8   A Load of Bull 36

9   Grandpa 2 - Germany 0 40

10 Clarrie gets into Trouble 48

11 The Plane 54

12 Christmas Party 58

13 Hedley Goes to War 65

14 The Football Match 74

15 Black Butter 83

16 Cousin Clara 95

17 Mother of the Free 106

– 1940 –

CHAPTER ONE

Land of Hope and Glory

The leathery skin around the deep blue eyes creased as the old man stared at the horizon. The clear sunny day and the shimmering calm blue sea made the nearby coast of France stand out like a sleeping giant. The only sound which interrupted his thoughts came from the birds, busy building their nests. Life for them would go on regardless of who controlled this small speck of land. They would be free to raise their family, then fly away whenever they so desired. For the human inhabitants of this dot on the earth's surface there would soon be a major decision to make. The old man sighed. He was standing on his land. His whole life was wrapped up in these few small parcels of grass and vegetation. Many larger landowners had tried to force him into selling his smallholding but no-one had managed to make him move and he was determined no-one ever would. Regardless of what his fellow islanders decided, he knew that when the time came he would fight tooth and nail for every inch of his property. Just like the mating birds, his family needed a future and this farm was it. Land of Hope and Glory went the words of his favourite song. This was his Land, his Hope for the future, and the Glory of his past years spent tilling the soil. Let them come. He would stay and fight.

The binoculars lowered to reveal a pair of hard steel blue eyes. So this was British soil. The long war finally seemed worthwhile. Thousands of his comrades had died to enable him to gaze upon the tiny speck of land in the distance. Only a few more miles and the first piece of British territory would be theirs. There was still some work to be done in France before the Fuhrer gave the order to advance across the sea. One or two towns were still offering resistance although it wouldn't take long to occupy the remaining areas, then they would be ready for the final onslaught. The stupid British with their Land of Hope and Glory. The Land would soon become part of Germany, no Hope for anyone who resisted, and Glory for the Third Reich.

CHAPTER TWO

The Ahier Family

The outbreak of World War II had been viewed by the islanders with dismay and a certain amount of trepidation. Dismay, with the fact that their fellow inhabitants of the globe couldn't manage to live in peace but constantly seemed to be at each other's throats. Trepidation, with the fact that this new beginning of hostilities amongst their neighbours might, in some unpleasant way, involve them. Many of the young, healthy and patriotic men sailed for England and joined the forces, but most Jerseymen continued working the land, hoping they would not be enslaved and believing that the States and honorary police would stop anyone interfering with the peaceful life on the farm.

As the Germans slowly made their way relentlessly through Europe, drawing ever closer to the nearby coast of France, the islanders smelt trouble. Jersey farmers can smell most things before they happen. Whether it be a storm, rain or long periods of sunny weather. A death in the family, a cow going down sick or the neighbours unmarried daughter getting pregnant. The farmer's nose seems to predict these things long before they materialize. News from the radio and a certain, indefinable smell in the air, told the locals something was about to happen to change their way of life.

In the far northwest of the island is the sleepy parish of St. Ouen, where the people carry on the work of the land. The parish consisted mainly of fields with a few houses, these being old granite farms, a quaint church, a couple of small shops and a local pub. In the neat, well laid out fields, herds of the beautiful Jersey cow graze peacefully in the quiet countryside. Jersey slopes from north to south therefore receives maximum benefit from the sun, also her shores are washed by the waters of the gulf stream enabling the island to enjoy milder winters and warmer summers than the mainland. Snow is rare, even in the coldest winter, so the animals lead a pleasant life. They are usually tethered to the ground with long chains or ropes. This is necessary as the fields are small and grass valuable. The Jerseyman, with his unusual sense of humour, will explain to any visitor who enquires, that the cattle are chained down because the farmers are fed up with travelling over to France to retrieve them whenever there are high winds.

St. Ouen, of all the parishes, is undoubtedly the farming backbone of the island and the locals have never taken kindly to outsiders coming into their parish. It used to be said that you needed a passport to enter and the luck of the devil to get out again. Stories have been told of boys from the big city of St. Helier who had tried to court the girls from St. Ouen. After escorting the young lady home, he would have to run the gauntlet to escape from the parish as the local boys would be waiting in ambush on the main exit roads. The farming families are extremely close, all working together on their farms. Once a week, normally on a Saturday, the family take the long trek into town to do the weekly shopping. The trip would be made either with the horse and cart or on the one bus a day, which managed to reach the outlying areas of the parish. One such family was the Ahier family.

Grandpa Ahier had lived at High View farm all his seventy-seven years, as had his father and his father's father. In fact there had been an Ahier living at High View as far back as the parish records went. His short, round shouldered, thin frail frame was deceptive. Underneath the rough, wrinkled leathery skin was a strong wiry man. His capacity for hard work showed up many of the younger generation, leaving them standing in his wake as his rough hands kept up a constant pace which his stubborn nature refused to allow him to slacken. His bright, piercing blue eyes were capable of out staring any man in an argument and no-one crossed him twice. Grey hair surrounded his bald crown which was permanently covered with an old cloth cap. A small straight nose, slightly furrowed near the bridge where his reading glasses rested, gave way to a thin, tight lipped mouth, where his remaining decaying teeth could be seen on the few occasions he managed a smile. Years of working outdoors in all weather had given his skin a ruddy complexion with a texture as hard as the local granite. He was slightly hard of hearing, although his cantankerous nature made good use of this disability by only hearing what he wanted to hear. Smartness in dress had never been one of Grandpa's good points. His clothes had seen better days and he could never understand why they had to be packed away every night just to be brought out the following morning. Grubby shirt collars and cuffs, baggy trousers, and torn crumpled jackets were a feature of Grandpa's clothing. His wife always maintained he would be rich if he could grow potatoes in the ground, like he grew them in his socks. The old man would turn his deaf ear to her complaints. Dressed like this he felt comfortable. Only on a Sunday would he allow his wife to lay out a clean shirt, a matching tie which he hated wearing, his best suit which was starting to shine from years of pressing, and a clean pair of shoes to replace his gumboots. Accordingly attired he would be marched off to church where his thin crackling voice could be heard, always at least two words behind the remainder of the congregation, singing the appointed hymns.

He spent every minute of his working day chewing on a stick of black tobacco, stopping every so often to spit out the offending juice. Even though he spoke good English, his main language was the old Jersey French patois which originates from the Norman French. Most of the country folk spoke this patois, finding it handy on market days when they wished to converse with another farmer without the town people understanding them. All Jersey farmers by tradition are poor. Grandpa Ahier being no exception, constantly complaining that the small farm was losing money. He had a mixed farm, the animal stock was made up of eight cows, four pigs, an old horse, one billy goat, some chickens and one bad tempered bull. Two dogs were kept, not just as pets, but to help control the dozens of rats who lived in the hay loft. A large field was kept in grass for the cows where Grandpa had planted apple trees when he was a boy which enabled him to make his own farm cider. He also had three other fields which were used for crops such as potatoes, tomatoes and broccoli. He kept no farm machinery, using the horse to do all the work. He believed these new fangled contraptions not only cost too much money but would never last. They kept breaking down whereas the horse didn't. For Grandpa, life consisted of working seven days a week. Saturday night he would allow himself the luxury of wandering down to the local with his fellow farmers, to chat about old times over a pint and a game of dominoes. All in all he was a typical Jersey farmer of the old school, spending all his time saying how poor he was, how the weather was always wrong, that the States of Jersey were to blame for everything and it was time they bucked up their ideas and did something about helping the poor farmer.

Grandma Ahier had also spent all her life on a farm. In fact she had been born just a few miles down the road on her parents farm. She had attended the parish school, then worked on her father's farm until she married Edmund Ahier at St. Ouen's Parish Church. She was an excellent cook, specializing in all the local dishes such as ormers, beancrocks and Jersey wonders. She never smoked or drank except when she had a cold and even then only a mixture of honey, lemon, hot water and farm cider, all stirred with a red hot poker. Every night she sat in the large kitchen with her knitting, the front room was only used on special occasions. On the farm Grandpa might be the boss but in the house it was different. At first glance she appeared to be a plump homely person. Someone to tell all your troubles to, who would listen with an understanding ear, make the correct sympathetic noises and magically find the right solution to every problem. In reality she was sixteen stone of trouble. From her short, tightly curled grey hair down to her size seven shoes, she was a match for any man. Her sharp, quick tongue could cut through any argument in mid-sentence whilst her large ears seemed to be able to pick up the most inaudible whisper within one hundred yards. Everything about her was expansive. Her large brown eyes, although bespectacled, never missed a thing. Her bulbous nose could smell trouble or gossip a mile away and her wide lips could create a fearsome snarl, showing a perfect set of white false teeth. The heavy chin was partially covered with grey hair which she was always pulling out with tweezers. She had long stopped bothering about her figure. Her large breasts nearly reached her waist, which had also developed as if to make a platform to take the weight of her bosom. From the waist, the hips seemed to spread out even further and the pair of oversized legs were needed to hold the combined mass of fat in an upright position. She was still agile for her size and age and was feared by everyone on the farm. She ruled the family with an iron fist. No-one put a foot out of line. God help anyone who walked into the house without first removing their boots. The farm was slightly run down but inside it was spotless and she aimed to keep it that way. She always had a pot of steaming coffee on the range whilst the smell of her cooking would waft around the farm making everyone's mouth water with anticipation. Her main fault was being too nosey and wanting to know everyone's business. She spent many happy hours gossiping with the neighbours about someone or other. Nothing was safe from her prying, consequently no-one could keep a secret she didn't uncover. If any of the family wanted to keep a possession in the house without her finding out they had to hide it well because she knew all the secret places and searched them regularly.

Making up the household were the Ahier's two grandchildren, Clarrie and Millie. Their father, Phillip Ahier, had been killed in the First World War after which their mother had run off with an Irish farmworker. Grandpa declared this was the fault of the States for allowing foreigners into the island. Consequently the old couple had been left to bring up their two grandchildren. Clarrie, who was now twenty-seven, had long been described as uncontrollable by his grandparents. He had a roving eye for all the unmarried girls, also a few of the married ones received his attentions, making his reputation well known throughout the parish. With his strong tall physique and straight black hair, always well greased and groomed, Clarrie cut quite a dashing figure. Dark swarthy complexion, brown eyes and broad shoulders, the girls didn't stand a chance.

Clarrie was a creature of habit. His courting dance was well known and many bets had been placed on Saturday nights in the local when some unsuspecting young lady had taken Clarrie's eye. First a quick comb of the hair, check the tie, make certain no cigarette ash had fallen on his trousers, then he would make his subtle approach. As he nonchalantly strode towards his intended victim he would turn his head slightly to the left, his right profile being by far the most beautiful. Give the girl a flash of his strong white teeth, take a long pull on his cigarette and slowly blow a smoke ring which would rise above his head like a halo. Clarrie had learnt this trick at a young age and great expertise was required to attain a perfect finish. If there was a slight draught the smoke could be misdirected and the young lady would be reduced to fits of coughing with tears streaming down her cheeks. When the manoeuvre was successful, Clarrie imagined he looked like a Saint and the girls wouldn't be able to resist his heavenly embrace. By this time a complete silence would have settled over the whole bar. Every face would be sporting a grin and all eyes would be on the undisputed master at work. A final parting of his wide lips, another quick smile, then the well tried and rehearsed punch line. "How about you and me taking a little walk darling?"

Yes, Clarrie was a creature of habit. Habitually drinking. This had placed the start of a middle age spread around his waist at a young age. Habitually chatting up the girls. His only regret, life was too short to be able to satisfy them all. Habitually smoking. He had no need to take matches with him when he went to work in the mornings as he chain smoked regardless of what duty he was performing. A fact that didn't go down too well with the cows when he did the milking. Habitually trying to dodge work. Clarrie didn't approve of the old methods of farming. He was full of new ideas on how the farm should be run but Grandpa never agreed with him, always out-voting his schemes at the family meetings. This made Clarrie discontented with his life on the small farm. He had grand ideas of starting up his own farm with all the latest modern methods and machinery. The only thing stopping him was the lack of funds. Clarrie was firmly stuck in a rut. Until something happened to Grandpa he could see no change of fortune on his horizon, and the old man reckoned he was going to live forever.

His sister Millie was totally different. She was four years younger than Clarrie, and Grandma had kept a close watch on her during her adult life. Not only wasn't she allowed out at night but any young man who dared to call would receive a few strong words from Grandma, then be seen off the premises by the two dogs. Millie was a carbon copy of her mother. Tall in stature, with long auburn hair, brown eyes and a fresh, unspoilt complexion. She was the apple of her Grandmother's eye. Most of Clarrie's friends had tried their hand at courting Millie but her full red lips were still pure and innocent of any male involvement. Her face would have carried away most beauty competition titles. A small, pert upturned nose gave a mischievous slant to the otherwise beautiful features. She was constantly looking in the mirror and worrying about lines appearing on her face and neck before she had any opportunity of capturing a husband. She showed off her long slim legs to their best advantage by shortening all her skirts and dresses. Grandma didn't approve but saw no harm as long as she could keep Millie out of reach of the male population. No Irish farmworker was going to steal away her little girl. She was well built although her hips were running a little on the heavy side. This was due to an excess of Grandma's home cooking and not enough exercise. She had never been allowed to develop any bad habits like drinking or smoking. The closest she was permitted to alcohol was a small glass of wine with her Christmas dinner. She once stole one of Clarrie's cigarettes but had been so sick she never tried smoking again. She sat at home every night waiting for a handsome young knight to arrive, charm Grandma, control two fierce dogs, then carry her away on his trusty farm horse.

The only other person who could be seen around the farm was Hedley. He was the village idiot and for some years had been employed by Grandpa to help with the odd jobs around the farm. A tall, gangling, gawky, young man, Hedley was the subject of much leg pulling and ridicule amongst the local youths. His cause wasn't helped by his squinting blue eyes, crooked nose, a legacy from a childhood fight, and the prominent wart on his chin. His endeavour to hide it by growing a blonde stubble only highlighted its presence. He walked around with a permanent grin which showed his broken, decayed teeth underneath a hair lip. This impediment caused his speech to be slow, stuttering, and difficult to understand. His intelligence was limited whilst his manner of dress left much to be desired. No matter the weather, Hedley always dressed the same. Gum boots, a pair of trousers that were three sizes too big for him but had been a bargain at the local jumble sale. A checked shirt and an old hat pulled down over his eyes completed his outfit. His parents had died when he was a boy leaving him uncertain as to his age but at a rough guess Grandpa put him at thirty-five. He had been shunted from pillar to post until unofficially adopted by the Ahiers upon his expulsion from school. He spent all day doing odd jobs in exchange for free board and lodgings. A few shillings in his pocket each week was enough to keep him in chewing gum, which he always had in his mouth, and one pint of beer on Saturday. Poor Hedley had one problem. Whenever he saw Millie he would get a strange feeling in his groin that was never there when he looked at the other people on the farm. He had never quite been able to work out the reason so decided he would have to ask Grandpa for an explanation.

Somehow this ill-matched group of people, thrown together by a German bullet, an Irish farmworker and years of interbreeding, managed to muddle through, scraping a small profit out of the farm. If anything went wrong, Hedley took the blame, receiving a kick from Grandpa. Season followed season without too many changes and would probably have continued to do so had it not been for the distant rumbling somewhere in Germany. This was causing the locals to listen carefully to their radios every night, even changing the topic of conversation in the local pub at weekends. War clouds hung on the horizon and that meant changes, and changes on the farm were never welcome. But then it was up to the States to put a stop to this maniac who was trying to take over the world.

CHAPTER THREE

Enter the Germans

Church that Sunday had not been the usual happy gathering of souls. A quiet foreboding had affected everyone, including the Ahier family. It was the 9th of June 1940, and on that day a pall of smoke had drifted over the island from France about noon, hanging around all day. The Allied armies were burning their dumps whilst on the retreat. The Germans were close. Grandpa sensed that panic would soon set in. Sunday evening they all sat in the front room. A special occasion. Maybe they wouldn't be around to use it much longer so they may as well enjoy the luxury whilst they could. Once the grandchildren had gone to bed Grandpa decided to bury the family silver.

"If the Germans come here I want to make certain they don't lay their hands on my bits and pieces."

Best to bury them at night so the children wouldn't know where they were, then the Germans wouldn't be able to torture them to find the family treasure. He gathered his few possessions and went outside. Millie was upstairs laying on her bed thinking along the same lines as her grandfather. All those men wanting to lay their hands on her bits and pieces filled her with anticipation and caused a smile to pass over her face. Grandma wouldn't be able to do anything about it because the Germans would probably force all the young girls to submit to their evil ways. She couldn't help wondering just how many men there were in an army. Good grief, she thought, this could be a full time job.

Spade in hand, Grandpa went into the back yard. He contemplated the best place to bury the silver. Choosing a spot behind the old barn he started digging but after a few moments struck something that sounded like glass. Carefully reaching down he picked up a bottle. Best bitter, it said on the label. There were dozens of them, all full. He covered them over and walked slowly back into the house.

"Clarrie, come down here at once."

Clarrie appeared in his underclothes, causing Grandma to blush and look quickly the other way.

"Right my boy, what are all those bottles doing buried outside?" .

"Why the Germans Grandpa. If they come we don't want to run out of beer, do we?"

The old man sighed. How was he supposed to understand a boy like this?

"Okay son, will you please tell me where I can do a spot of digging without disturbing your hidden treasure?"

Clarrie thought for a few moments. He went over all the places he had hidden drink and cigarettes.

"Well come on boy, there must be one or two places left you haven't used."

Clarrie's face suddenly lit up. "You could try the bottom end of number two field."

"Good God, how much have you got buried out there?"

Clarrie's brow creased in concentration. "Well let me see. There's a few hundred cases of beer and about two thousand fags. I've spent all my savings on them."

Grandpa shook his head. All the boy could think about was drinking, cigarettes and girls.

"You haven't got any females buried out there, have you?"

Clarrie smiled. "Don't be silly Grandpa, they would suffocate under ground."

"Go to bed son, I've got some work to do. Number two field you said?"

Clarrie looked puzzled. "What do you want to bury Grandpa?"

"Why your grandmother of course. I can't let the Germans get their hands on her, now can I?"

The skin around his eyes crinkled into a grin. He seldom cracked a joke or put one over on his grandson and it made him feel good.

"Goodnight boy, pleasant dreams."

The next few days seemed to drag by. News kept coming through of the German advance and on the 12th of June it was reported that they had taken Paris. Grandpa tried not to look worried and alarm the rest of the household.

"Never mind. When they try to invade the islands the British will push them back into the sea."

But on the 17th, with heavy gunfire coming from France, it was decided the islands would be evacuated of all troops and left defenceless. All the British soldiers who had dug themselves in around the island would be sent to fight on another front. That night everyone had to leave the pub early as a curfew had been imposed at nine o'clock. There had been a great deal of discussion about the withdrawal of the British troops. The wise old heads could understand it was really for the best, because if they had stayed the Germans would have blown the island out of the water. Some of the youngsters wanted to form their own army and fight the Germans with shotguns and pitchforks but were told by their elders not to be so stupid. Clarrie was busy burying some more beer when he dug up the family silver and when trying to rebury it he dug up a box of cigarettes. Eventually he managed to get everything underground but couldn't remember each items exact location. Thousands of people were leaving the island before the Germans arrived, being taken to England by boat. A debate took place during the evening as to the future of the Ahier family. Grandpa aired his views first.

"We've just got the farm straight and Bessie the cow is expecting. Besides which, I'm too old to start again in a foreign land so I'm going to stay."

Grandma thought the children should go but they were both adamant they wouldn't go without their grandparents. Also Clarrie wouldn't leave without his buried hoard of treasure, so in the end it was decided everyone would stay on the farm and make the best of it. After all, it was up to the States to see the local people were protected from the enemy.

They didn't have long to wait, for on the 1st of July, the Germans arrived, having first dropped leaflets telling the people to drape white flags everywhere as a sign of surrender. Grandpa placed a sheet over the fence and Clarrie hoisted his best white shirt up a pole. Grandma refused to show or wear anything white. Millie, thinking she should enter into the spirit of the moment, hung her underclothes out on the line. Grandma soon pulled them in. The bra and panties were only giving Hedley a headache. The poor man had spent an hour staring at these strange white garments, trying to work out what they could possibly be used for. So the occupation had started and life would now be different for the plain simple country folk down on the farm.

– 1940 –

CHAPTER FOUR

Rules and Regulations

Clarrie was not impressed. The list of rules and regulations posted by the Germans included a curfew between the hours of 11pm and 6am. This would have a disastrous effect on his love life. How could he manage to keep all his young ladies satisfied during the few hours between finishing work on the farm and 11pm. After all, farming was a seven day a week job and Grandpa only allowed him one weekend off a month. Some of the girls would have to be disappointed. He decided to make a list of his favourites and concentrate all his time and affection on these few special females. He realized it would be hard on the ones left out but, in the months ahead, everyone had to make sacrifices. Maybe Hedley could help him out with some of the left overs? No, maybe not. It would mean taking the chewing gum out of his mouth and he most certainly would require a crash course on how to handle women.

The Germans had ordered all spirits to be locked up and therefore removed from sale in public houses, this did not include any stocks in private houses. Clarrie was still able to go to the local for a pint of beer, but how long would that last? He decided to keep his large stock buried, in case the occupation continued for a long time. If stocks in the pub ran out, he would be able to dig up some beer and have a constant supply for his own consumption, plus enough left over to sell to certain friends at a profit

Grandpa had been sly. Whilst Clarrie was busy burying beer, the old man had stored a case of brandy in the cellar under the kitchen, strictly for medicinal purposes of course. Grandpa suffered a great deal from stomach trouble and always had a small brandy on these occasions. Grandma was convinced his trouble came from overeating but the old man insisted he couldn't help himself because she was such a good cook, besides which, he needed to eat to maintain his strength to manage all the heavy farmwork. Load of rubbish, thought Clarrie. The old boy just likes a tipple now and again so he uses his stomach as an excuse.

Another rule concerned all rifles, airguns, pistols, revolvers, daggers, sporting guns and all other weapons whatsoever, except souvenirs, with all ammunition, which had to be handed over to the Germans. Most farmers owned some sort of gun, mainly shotguns, which they used on the rabbit population. The Ahier's owned two such weapons and one was duly handed over together with half the ammunition, whilst the remaining gun and ammunition was placed in the cellar by Grandpa as a souvenir of his hunting days. A heavy rug was spread over the trap door to the cellar successfully hiding it. The old man also stored numerous other articles down there which he felt might come in handy during a long occupation.

The Germans, on the whole, appeared to treat the local people well, but it was early days and many folk were convinced harder times were ahead, especially if the occupation proved to be lengthy. The Germans were already buying great quantities of food, clothing and innumerable other items from the shops using their occupation marks. These were specially minted coins and notes called Reichskredit currency. Used only in countries occupied by the Germans, they were worthless elsewhere, and consisted of zinc coins of 1,2,5, and 10 Reichspfennigs, and notes of 50 Reichspfennigs as well as notes of 1,2,5,20 and 50 Reichmarks. Eventually all British currency disappeared, everyone being forced to use the new notes. The rate of exchange was fixed at 9.36 Reichmarks to the Pound, therefore 1 Mark was equal to 2 shillings and 1½d.

Wireless sets could be kept but Grandpa was amongst many people who forecast that this law would eventually be changed, so the wireless also found its way into the cellar. They had the old gramophone to amuse themselves with at night and Grandpa always maintained the old proverb "Early to bed, early to rise, makes a man happy, healthy and wise" was true. As they all had to be up early in the mornings, the whole family could retire to bed a little earlier than usual. Clarrie was not impressed.

– 1941 –

CHAPTER FIVE

Visitors

"We need more hay down from the loft" Grandpa called out to Hedley. "Throw me down a bundle, I'll carry it over to the stable."

Hedley didn't like heights, also the ladder was old and rickety. He climbed carefully, slowly disappearing into the loft. Grandpa stood beneath waiting. Good God, what was keeping the boy?

"Hurry up Hedley, there's no time to have a sleep in the hay."

A bundle of hay suddenly appeared and fell down at the old man's feet. He picked up his fork and was just about to push it into the bundle when there was a cry from above. Something came hurtling down from the loft, landing with a thud on top of the hay.

"You stupid idiot. I might have stuck the fork into you."

He kicked the unfortunate man, stopping suddenly, mouth open, when he saw Hedley appear at the top of the ladder. Who on earth was he kicking?

"Who are you? What are you doing in my hay loft?"

The body picked itself up off the ground. The unshaven, ill kept man rubbed his backside where the old man's boot had left its mark.

"Don't I know you?" inquired Grandpa, staring at the intruder.

Beneath the crumpled, bedraggled clothes and stubbled chin was a tall, sandy haired young man of about twenty eight. Large blue eyes stared back at Grandpa from out of a grimy, unwashed face.

"Yes Mr. Ahier. I'm Bill Pallot. I used to live in the village before I joined up."

"Joined up with what?"

"The British Army sir. I've been sent back as a spy."

"A spy?" The old man looked puzzled. "What do you expect to find in my hay loft? German soldiers."

"No sir. I was hiding up there. I couldn't go back home. The rest of my family evacuated before the occupation, so the house was left empty, now its been taken over by the Germans."

"Hedley, keep your chewing gum firmly between your teeth and tell no-one about this. You, inside quick before anyone sees you."

"Mother, have you any coffee on the stove? We've got a visitor who's in need of a hot drink." The old man pushed Bill Pallot into the large kitchen, hurriedly closing the door. Grandma was too busy over the range to look up.

"There's some on the table that's still hot" she called over her shoulder.

Bill Pallot sat down whilst Grandpa poured the coffee.

"Now tell me what this is all about?"

Just then Grandma finished her preparing and turned around.

"What are you doing here? I told you never to let me see your face around here again." She picked up her rolling pin making straight towards Bill. The dogs sensed trouble, growled and moved behind Grandma to give her support. Bill, who had already been kicked several times by Grandpa, was now about to be attacked by his wife. He leapt off his chair, making straight for the door. The dogs beat him to it, trapping him between them and Grandma, who was advancing fast.

The old man caught hold of his wife's arm. "What the hell has got into you woman?"

Grandma's piercing eyes were fixed firmly on the soldier. "This is the young man I caught last year outside the back door with our Millie."

Grandpa remembered him now. The last time he had seen Bill was when Grandma had chased him all round the farmyard with her rolling pin. Bill had tried to escape on his pushbike but the dogs had brought him crashing down into the manure heap. The old man placed himself between his wife and the unfortunate soldier.

"This is different Ma. He's a British soldier now and has been sent to spy on the Germans. He was using our hayloft as cover until Hedley found him. We must help him in any way we can."

Grandma lowered her rolling pin although she continued glaring at Bill, not certain whether to believe the story. At that precise moment the kitchen door flew open as Clarrie and Millie walked in.

Clarrie looked at Bill in surprise. "Hello Bill, what are you doing here? I thought you joined up."

Millie was even more surprised and delighted at seeing Bill again. After the beating he had received on his last visit, she hadn't expected him to return. Grandpa explained to the youngsters who started asking questions on how the war was progressing and when the British troops would be returning. Grandma was calming down, although she decided to keep an eye on this young man, as her female intuition warned her against trusting Bill anywhere near Millie. Still he needed hot food and no-one in need ever left her kitchen hungry. She went over to the range where a large saucepan of home made soup was boiling. Clarrie dug up a crate of beer to celebrate, whilst Hedley offered a stick of his precious chewing gum. Grandpa thought a drop of brandy would be appreciated by all concerned. Millie could think of nothing she could offer except to undo the top two buttons of her blouse.

The old man noticed the soldier was shivering. "Get out of those wet things, Clarrie will find you something warm to wear."

Bill Pallot had already finished his first bowl of soup, he was hungrily tucking into his second helping whilst thinking to himself that Millie's dumplings would make an enjoyable sweet.

Grandpa interrupted his train of thought. "You can stay with Hedley. There's a spare bed in his room. We'll help you all we can but you must keep out of sight of the Germans until it's time for you to be picked up."

"That's not for another two days. I need to make a reconnaissance of the airport to check the number of planes."

Grandpa thought it would be a dangerous mission until Hedley pointed out if Bill borrowed his bike then, disguised in Clarrie's clothes, he should be alright. So it was settled. Bill would sleep with Hedley, travel to the airport in the morning, then lay low until it was time to leave. After a late dinner, the evening was spent talking around the fire. Grandpa disclosed all the information he knew about the Germans and their treatment of the local inhabitants. As they were going to bed, Grandma suggested one of the dogs should sleep in Hedley's room and guard them. She was really thinking of dissuading Bill from making any advances towards Millie. Bill reluctantly went to bed accompanied by one watchful dog, who kept one eye open all night in case he made the slightest move towards Millie's room.

The following morning started with the four men enjoying a hearty breakfast. Grandma kept Millie busy with enough chores for her to remain well out of Bill's reach. Added to which, the watch dog lay near the commando's feet, following his every movement. Curse the bloody thing, thought Bill. Doesn't this dog ever sleep. Grandpa saw everything but said nothing. He liked Bill. The lad came from a good local family. It was time to allow Millie more freedom. Grandma had kept her wrapped in cotton wool for long enough, still thinking of her as a little girl, not as a grown woman with feelings and needs.

Breakfast over, the men started working out their plan of action for the day. Clarrie had found some suitable clothes, including an old hat that would cover most of Bill's face. Hedley had parked his bike outside, even remembering to pump the tyres up. Bill was just about to leave when Hedley came rushing back into the house.

"The sow had her piglets during the night boss. There's eight of them."

Everyone went outside to the pigsty. The proud sow was on her side feeding her young, hungry bunch of children. The Germans had ordered every farmer to inform the States vet when piglets were born, enabling him to come out and count the young. A German soldier would always be present on these occasions. Grandpa knew he would have to fill in various forms, also answer numerous questions, as to whether he intended to keep, sell or kill the piglets.

"You'd better be off before the vet and his pet German arrive. When you return be careful in case they're still around."

Grandpa shook Bill's hand, watched him climb onto Hedley's bike and wobble off towards the main road.

"That's a plucky lad. He'll probably be shot if the Germans catch him yet he acts like he hasn't a care in the world. Right Clarrie, I'm going to phone the vet, you take three of the piglets and hide them somewhere in the house out of the way."

The family trooped back into the house leaving Clarrie to select three of the plumpest piglets. Once the vet, with his German guard, had made the count, the young pigs could be returned to their mother.

Grandpa made his phone call then turned to his wife. "He's coming this morning. Old Ted Carre from Longfield Farm has a sick cow, so as he's out this way he'll fit us in on the same journey."

"I'll make certain there's plenty of coffee on" Grandma moved towards the range. The dog who had been guarding Bill during the night had finally dropped off to sleep, choosing a warm position by the range. Grandma, in a rush as usual, didn't see the dog. She tripped over him, landing on the floor with a crash which shook the whole house. The old man rushed to his wife and tried to lift her.

"It's my shoulder. I caught it on the range as I fell."

Grandma was too stunned to regain her feet by herself, even the joint efforts of her husband and Millie were insufficient to lift her. Clarrie entered just at the right moment, his arms full of piglets.

"Quick, give me a hand to lift your grandmother."

Clarrie handed the piglets to Millie and picked Grandma up without any effort. He placed her into the armchair by the window whilst Grandpa opened his brandy bottle and poured out a stiff measure.

"Here mother, drink this, it will calm you down."

Grandma didn't realize what she was doing. She raised the glass to her lips, took a sip of brandy, immediately collapsing into a fit of coughing as the neat spirit reached her throat.

"What are you trying to do, kill me? I've only hurt my shoulder."

Grandpa didn't believe in waste so he knocked back the rest of the brandy in one mouthful.

"Just to make certain I'll phone the doctor."

Grandma didn't want the doctor to be called but the old man insisted, as he knew a fall at her age could incur complications.

"Seems we're going to have a busy morning" Grandpa replaced the phone. "The doctor agrees with me, he's coming out as soon as possible to check you over."

Clarrie had disappeared with the piglets, wondering where the best place would be to hide them. At that exact moment Bill Pallot walked in through the kitchen door.

"What are you doing back?" Grandpa looked worried."I got as far as the crossroads to find the place crawling with Germans. They were on some kind of exercise which included stopping everyone. I turned round and came straight back."

"Well this place is going to be crawling with people soon" Grandpa turned to Clarrie, who had came back into the kitchen on hearing Bill's voice. "You'd better find somewhere for him to hide as well."

The two men went off carrying the piglets. Where on earth could he hide this lot, thought Clarrie.

Work had to continue. Millie was left in charge of Grandma, whilst Clarrie and Hedley were sent to the fields to carry on their work. Grandpa had some urgent mending to do in the barn. Everyone went about their various jobs until the old man was interrupted by the sound of a car pulling into the farmyard. The short, dumpy figure of the States vet, accompanied by a German soldier, stepped out of the car and walked over to Grandpa.

"Good morning Mr. Ahier." The vet shook hands with Grandpa. They walked slowly across to the pigsty chatting about the weather and various problems the farmers were experiencing under the new German regulations. The soldier was ignored and left to follow behind like a spare part. The vet, on being told of the accident, was sympathetic about Grandma's fall, agreeing the best thing was to have called the doctor.

"You can't be too careful at her age, a fall could be dangerous."

After inspecting the sow and checking all five piglets, the vet produced a mass of paper work for Grandpa to fill in.

"I'm sorry about this, but there's nothing I can do. Rules and regulations must be followed. Food is starting to run short so they want to know the ins and outs of a cows backside. Everything that moves has to be accounted for."

"We'll fill these in over a cup of coffee" Grandpa led the vet towards the house. "I suppose you had better bring Fritz with you."

"No choice I'm afraid. He's like a shadow. I even have trouble going to the toilet without him."

Grandma was still sitting in the armchair when they entered the kitchen. The vet shook hands then sat talking to Grandma whilst Millie poured the coffee. The young German soldier stood stiffly to attention, keeping one hand on his rifle and one eye on the dogs. He had just arrived in the island and felt a misjustice had been dealt to him. He would have been better employed fighting the enemies of the fatherland. These people nauseated him. They had been prepared to hand over their island without any form of resistance. They were no longer worthy to be called men. He stood aloof, feeling himself to be one of the superior race made to suffer the company of cowards. He would never earn the iron cross in a place like this. The sound of another car pulling into the yard brought Grandpa to his feet.

"That'll be the doctor." He went over to the door and greeted the ageing family physician. Millie poured another cup of coffee, then to the annoyance of the German, they all started speaking in local patois.

"You vill speak in English"

"You will go to hell" replied Grandpa in Jersey French.

The doctor warmed his hands by the fire. A kindly old man who should have retired years ago, he had known the Ahier family most of his life. With this occupation there would be no chance of putting his feet up and spending the remaining years of his life pouring over his prize stamp collection. Many of the young doctors had left the island before the Germans had arrived so a great deal of work had now fallen on his shoulders. His hands were glowing. He never believed in examining anyone with cold fingers. Placing his small gold rimmed glasses on the end of his nose he moved over to inspect his patient.

"I would prefer your wife upstairs to examine her properly but she's having difficulty walking. Is Clarrie around to help?"

Grandpa shook his head. "He's down the field with Hedley, but I can call him."

"No need for that" volunteered the vet. "The German can help me carry her upstairs."

Grandma wasn't too keen having a German handling her and he wasn't happy having to put down his rifle or touch one of these spineless, weak-hearted people. Eventually, after a great deal of struggling from the men and cursing from Grandma, they finally layed her on the bed.

"Now let me have a good look at that shoulder" The doctor moved over to the side of the bed.

"I'm not taking my clothes off in front of him" snorted Grandma, pointing at the German.

The doctor smiled. "Thank you gentlemen. I think I can manage from here. If you could please close the door after you."

"Where's your dressing gown my dear. I'll fetch it for you whilst you slip your dress off."

"It's in the wardrobe, but how can I undress? I can hardly move."

The vet turned back into the room. "You know me well enough Mrs. Ahier. Perhaps you'll allow me to help you."

"Very well, but the German must wait outside."

The vet moved over to the bed and helped the old lady slip off her dress whilst the doctor went to the wardrobe to find her dressing gown. He reached into the wardrobe and turned quickly around. The vet had his back to him and was busy with Grandma. The doctor pulled the dressing gown off the peg, then firmly closed the wardrobe door.

"It's alright, I can manage her now. Thank you for your help."

Both the vet and the old lady were red in the face and the poor man was only too pleased to be able to leave the room. Animals never gave him this amount of trouble.

Back downstairs the German was furious to find Millie holding his rifle. As he moved quickly towards her the dogs made a dive for him and caught the back of his trousers. A ripping sound caused him to yell and kick out at the dogs. Grandpa barked an order, calling the dogs sheepishly back to their corner.

"I'm sorry about that" claimed Grandpa, trying not to laugh. "They must have thought you were going to attack my grand-daughter."

"If you take off your trousers I'll mend them for you" volunteered Millie.

The poor soldier didn't know what to do. To take off his trousers in front of these people would be degrading, but to report back to his sergeant with torn trousers would land him in trouble. The former seemed to be the lesser of the two evils. He removed his trousers and stood stiffly to attention in his long underpants, still clutching hold of his rifle.

Clarrie, having finished his work in the field, returned to the farmyard to find two cars parked there. He made straight for the kitchen, bursting in to find his grandfather and the vet drinking coffee, Millie sitting down with a pair of trousers in her hand, and a German soldier, with a red face, standing in the corner minus his pants.

"Nothing unusual ever happens in this place" Clarrie grinned at the German. "Been caught with your trousers down, have you? Where's Grandma and the doctor?"

"Upstairs in the bedroom" replied Grandpa. "We had a job to get her there but the two men helped."

The old man stared at Clarrie whose face had gone white. The vet had also noticed the colour of Clarrie's face.

"Don't worry. She'll be alright. The doctor checked there was nothing broken before he allowed us to carry her upstairs. It will just be a bad case of bruising."

The doctor, having finished his examination of Grandma, walked in at that moment. He also had to smile at the sight of the German soldier. As soon as Millie finished her mending the poor man quickly restored his dignity. He knew it wouldn't take long for the story to be circulated and if his fellow soldiers found out he would become the laughing stock of the German army.

The vet turned to the German. "Time we were going. If your battle dress is in perfect order, we've got two more calls to make. Be careful at the next place, they keep a vicious canary."

He smiled and shook hands all round. "Thank you for an interesting call. The remainder of the day is going to seem dull after this visit."

Grandpa saw him to the door. The German took one last look at the dogs who seemed to be smiling at him. Whoever said animals were dumb. The doctor sat quietly in the armchair lighting his pipe. He puffed away until he heard the sound of the car move off down the road.

"Now maybe someone can tell me why there is a man in the wardrobe holding three piglets?"

Grandpa turned to Clarrie. "You stupid idiot, you might have got us all shot."

"Don't worry" the doctor calmed Grandpa down. "I delivered Bill into this world and I'm not about to deliver him to the Germans. Now what's this all about?"

Grandpa explained whilst Clarrie rescued Bill out of the wardrobe, much to the surprise of Grandma. The doctor spent an hour with Bill telling him everything he knew. He was allowed considerable freedom as he could always say he was visiting a patient, so he was able to provide much useful information.

The remainder of Bill's stay passed without further incident. Although Grandma had to stay upstairs and rest, the dogs made certain Bill and Millie were never alone. At last the time came for him to leave. Everyone wished him luck. Millie gave him a kiss on the cheek whilst the dogs, their job over, licked his hand. Bill packed up his few belongings and said his goodbyes. On his way across the yard he stopped at the pigsty. He couldn't tell which piglets he had shared the wardrobe with, so he said goodbye to them all.

"This is one trip I'll never forget" Bill grinned at the assembled family. "I'll have a story to tell that will guarantee me free drinks in the mess for a month."

– 1941 –

CHAPTER SIX

The V Signs

The practice of painting V signs on buildings and prominent walls soon became a popular pastime amongst the local youngsters. Even some elders of the community had been seen with the odd pot of paint in their hands. V signs first appeared in the town of St. Helier, then spread rapidly to all four corners of the island. The Germans decided to counteract these victory slogans with stiff punishments. Anyone caught painting the offending signs would be sent to prison for nine months, also all wireless sets in the area where the culprit lived were confiscated. This didn't dampen the spirits of the artistic population. More large white signs appeared nightly, with few of those responsible being caught.

The farmers of St. Ouen had better things to do with their time than paint silly signs everywhere. They understood the meaning, sympathized with the cause, but didn't have the time to be involved. Farming was a seven day a week job with little time left over to mess about with pots of paint. Besides which, paint cost money, money was scarce, so if a farmer bought paint it most certainly didn't go onto any wall, apart from his own farmhouse. The States should supply free paint to those who wished to daub V signs in retaliation to the German occupation.

June 15th, 1941, the parish hall of St. Ouen had, during the previous evening, been attacked by an unknown person armed with a paint brush and a pot of white paint. The V sign on the door of the hall was duly inspected by German and local alike. A definite work of art. Thick broad lines, with the paint being liberally applied. Officials of the parish rolled up their sleeves and started mopping-up operations. No-one had been seen painting the offending sign so no charges could be brought. As to the confiscation of wireless sets, the officials argued that, as the Germans couldn't prove someone from around the immediate area was responsible, no wireless sets should be taken from the locals. The Germans allowed the argument to stand though issued a stiff warning that if it happened again the locals would be held responsible.

The locals heeded the warning. All wireless sets disappeared overnight. A farm is an easy place to hide something small. Farmers being ingenious, hid their sets in places the Germans would never think of looking. Ted Carre from Longfields, had dug up his manure heap, placed his wireless set in a tin box, then piled all the cow manure on top. It would only be for a week until whoever was painting these signs was caught. Grandpa still had his wireless set down in the cellar under the kitchen. He would bring it up once a night for about half an hour to listen to the news then take it straight back. Without the set in the kitchen to listen to at night, the family collection of records was starting to wear out. Each individual had their favourite records which would be played constantly during the long evenings. Grandma tried teaching the children to dance. Millie thought it was wonderful, she would be able to go dancing when all this trouble was over. Clarrie thought it was stupid. Why waste time dancing with a girl? He spent his spare time learning to play his harmonica. Although he may not be able to sing outside a young girl's bedroom, he could play soft music to woo her into his arms. Hedley even tried the harmonica but his chewing gum kept getting stuck in the holes. Grandpa had a theory about the V signs. He reckoned it was the work of a town boy who was trying to retaliate against the locals for not allowing him to court a farmer's daughter. Grandma decided it was a farmer whose daughter had been interfered with by the Germans. Clarrie wanted to know more about the daughter. Millie wanted to be interfered with.

The second V sign appeared outside the little corner shop. This time the Germans searched all the houses in the district, coming up with only three wireless sets. These had been left on tables or sideboards in full view of the soldiers. All three sets hadn't worked for years. The owners felt it was better for the Germans to find a few sets to confiscate rather than search the area fruitlessly. Also it saved the farmer the job of disposing of the wireless himself. Still no sign of the culprit could be found. Whoever it was had been extremely clever. Some of the farmers sided with the Germans because they sensed trouble. They could see if this man was allowed to persist, the soldiers might think of some stiffer penalties.

The first two signs had been painted during the early evening. The third appeared during the day. Grandpa was not amused. The wall of his farmhouse bordering the main road had been daubed with white paint. The Germans came to view the sign. The old man seemed more angry than they were. He offered a dozen eggs to the officer in charge if he could bring the culprit to justice.

"I don't care if this maniac paints signs all over the island but not on my property" Poor Hedley received a kick and was sent to scrub the offending paint off the wall. The Germans were given such a verbal onslaught by Grandpa, they ended up apologizing to him for the V sign.

"Vee Vill try to see it never happens again" promised the officer.

The interview had been a difficult one. The old man constantly shouting about his property, Grandma sitting in the corner with her rolling pin at the ready, two dogs waiting for him to turn his back or make a wrong move and Millie, smiling at him the whole time. What a strange nation. He couldn't understand why it was taking so long for the Imperial German Army to conquer England if this was a sample of the population. He ordered his men back to the search, his mind somewhere between Millie and a dozen eggs.

Grandma needed some groceries from the little shop opposite the church. Clarrie would be needed to help carry them. He didn't mind at all. Firstly, it meant he could leave the job of cleaning out the cow stalls to Hedley. Secondly, he would be able to see the girl who worked in the small shop. The horse and cart was made ready for the short journey. For once the horse seemed quite happy about doing some work, usually Clarrie had a terrible job with him. The horse and Hedley had a great deal in common - both were lazy and both were always chewing.

The little shop was extremely low on stock. The Germans requisitioned all the goods they required, leaving only a small amount for the locals. Grandma spent half an hour searching the shelves for any item they may have overlooked. Clarrie spent his time chatting to the girl behind the counter. Yes, she was free next Sunday after church to go for a walk. We won't walk far promised Clarrie. Down by the old mill he knew a few places where a young couple could spend a pleasant hour.

"Come on Clarrie, time to go. Bring your eyes and hands with you. The young lady has work to do" Grandma handed him a large box to load onto the cart.

"Drive round the back of the church. I'll meet you inside after I've had a chat with Mrs. Le Feuvre. A session of prayer will do you good. I want to see the vicar about the flower arrangements for next Sunday."

Clarrie disappeared, his business with the young girl completed. He would wander around the back of the church and go inside when he saw his grandmother approaching.

The German patrol came from the direction of St. Ouen's bay. Clarrie noticed them as they reached the top of the hill. He rushed into church, then knelt down in the back pew pretending to pray. Grandma slumped down beside him. She crossed herself and prayed quietly. She hated the Germans. Clarrie knew she would be praying for something to happen to make the soldiers disappear. He smiled to himself and carried on praying for an endless supply of girls. The doorway of the church was suddenly filled with Germans. The half a dozen people who were in church stopped their praying, turned towards the door and stared at the soldiers who were looking around at the gathering. It was the same officer who had visited the house about the V sign. He marched up the aisle, glancing from side to side.

"You are in the house of the Lord" whispered Grandma. "Remove your hat and lay down your weapons."

The German turned, recognised Mrs. Ahier, gave a sharp bow and took off his cap.

"My apologies Madam. My manners have failed me." He gave a signal to his men who also removed their helmets but kept their rifles at the ready.

"Somevone has painted a V sign on zee vall outside zee church. Zee paint is still vet. I vish zat person to come forward now."

No-one moved. The vicar came down the aisle and faced the officer.

"Do you come to church in peace my son?"

The German crossed himself. "Nien Fazer. Someone has defiled your church by painting a V sign on zee vall. I vant zat person."

"Do you think any of these ladies would do such a thing?" The vicar looked around the church.

"Nien. But I vould like to question zat young man over zere."

Clarrie froze. He'd only been playing leap frog over the

27

gravestones. Surely the Germans couldn't think he would paint signs on the wall.

"This young man is with me" muttered Grandma. "He's been with me the whole time in the shop across the road and whilst I've been praying."

"Of course, I remember him from ven I visited your house. He's your grandson. Very vell, search zee church."

The Germans searched every inch to no avail. There was no-one hiding in the corners or behind any of the pews. One soldier, who had been sent to look outside, came in carrying a pot of paint.

"I found zis behind vun of zee gravestones."

The German officer bowed to the vicar. "It seems I vas wrong. Zee man must have run off as vee approached, leaving his paint behind. I vould like to visit your beautiful church again under more pleasant circumstances."

He glanced at Grandma. "I think vee vill meet again Madam."

With this he marched out taking his men with him. The vicar made the sign of the cross, then led everyone in a prayer for a speedy conclusion to the occupation.

Later that afternoon a loud knocking on the door brought Grandma out of her nap with a start. The men were down the fields working, Millie was upstairs doing the cleaning so she was left alone to answer the demanding knock. The old lady walked across to the door, outside in the farmyard stood the officer from the church.

"I have come for my dozen eggs. I don't think zee painter vill strike again."

Millie came downstairs. The German bowed to her. "Good afternoon young lady. It is a beautiful day, is it not?"

"Millie, go and fetch a dozen eggs out of the shed. This officer has found out who was responsible for painting the V signs. Your grandfather promised him the eggs so we must pay our debts."

Millie went into the shed where the precious eggs were kept. Fancy Grandpa being so rash as to promise the German a reward. He was normally tight. Besides they needed the eggs themselves. Still Grandpa was the boss. She counted out a dozen eggs, choosing the smallest ones possible. Coming back into the kitchen she handed the eggs to the officer. He bowed to both females, then turning to

Grandma he smiled. "I understand zat turps vill remove zee paint from zee skin,"

As he turned to leave he ended with a parting remark. "I hope zat I never have to come and visit you again madam. I suggest you paint your kitchen, it could do with it."

Millie couldn't follow what was going on but Grandma understood perfectly. How was she going to explain to her husband why she gave one dozen eggs to the German without the name of the culprit being mentioned. It was not going to be easy.

CHAPTER SEVEN

Grandpa 1 – Germany 0

It was the kind of morning when Clarrie wished work hadn't been invented. The sun shone out of a clear blue sky and a light breeze gently rustled the leaves on the trees. Just the type of day to go for a walk with a young lady on his arm, complete with a picnic from Grandma's kitchen. But there was a war on. Things were different now. Clarrie wished this occupation would come to a speedy conclusion, allowing life to return to normal. He lingered over his second cup of coffee wondering if the good old days would ever return. No-one thought the Germans would have been allowed to stay so long. Grandpa had been certain they would have been kicked out inside a month, but time was dragging on. They seemed to have been here for years. All these rules and regulations were ruining Clarrie's sex life. How could he possibly carry on normally when he had to be in so early at night. To complicate matters, Grandma wouldn't allow him to bring any young ladies over the threshold.

Grandpa interrupted his train of thought. "Take the horse and plough the bottom field."

Now the bottom field bordered the cliffs with just a hedge about twenty yards between the field and a sheer drop of several hundred feet straight down to the sea. It was by far the best place to work on a hot day, right away from everyone, with a good view of the other islands and the coast of France. With luck he would be able to have a nap sometime during the afternoon when the temperature was liable to rise into the eighties. He strolled across the farmyard to the stable. The horse didn't fancy the idea of working. He put up quite a struggle before Clarrie managed to get the halter on him. He kept shaking his head, trying to get the bit out of his mouth. In the end Clarrie won, though by now they were both starting to work up a sweat. If he had his way he would dispose of the horse, finding an easier way of doing the work. Blast Grandpa and his old fashioned ideas.

Slowly they made their way down towards the bottom field. Clarrie, wanting to get there quickly to enable him to finish the job and have a rest later and the horse not so keen because he didn't want to start work at all. At last Clarrie managed to manoeuvre him into the field, only to pull up sharply in surprise. Standing near the end of the field, alongside the hedge, were two Germans. They seemed to be measuring something. Clarrie was in a quandary. Should he carry on with his ploughing or go and investigate. Being inquisitive, he decided to reconnoitre the situation. Moving carefully down the field Clarrie made his way towards the Germans. The horse was becoming harder to pull as if he sensed trouble. The Germans had noticed Clarrie approaching and looked up as he came close to them. One wore the uniform of a junior officer, he was a large blonde man with a huge hooknose and a thick square jaw. At least 6ft 4ins of trouble. The other was a private who smiled at Clarrie. At least he seemed reasonably friendly.

Hooknose opened the conversation. "Good morgan. Can I help you?"

"I just wondered what you were doing in our field"

"Vee are marking out zee position for a bunker" replied Hooknose.

Clarrie scratched his head thoughtfully. "What do you want to store coal here for?"

"Coal. Nien, a bunker zat has a gun in it, so guarding any attack from zee sea" Hooknose raised his eyes to the heavens. What a simple lot these locals were.

"Zis is an ideal spot for a look out bunker for vee can see zee other islands and zee coast of France from here."

"But you can't build a bunker here, this is our best field for crops"

Clarrie wished his grandfather was with him to deal with these soldiers.

"Zat is unfortunate for you, but I'm under orders. Find zee best places for bunkers, mark zem out, zen build zem. Zis place is excellent, so vee vill be building vun here."

Hooknose then dismissed Clarrie and continued talking to his comrade in German. Clarrie's mind was in a whirl. What was he going to do? Find Grandpa quick, he would know how to stop these people digging a large hole in their field, burying loads of concrete, then inserting a gun that would make a great deal of noise and frighten the animals. Probably stop the chickens from laying their eggs.

"I'd better call my grandfather. He owns this field. I'm sure he won't like this."

Hooknose twisted his already unfriendly face into a leer. "Too bad. But go ahead and call him anyvay. It von't make any difference. Vee are going to build here vhether you and your grandfather like it or not."

Clarrie ran up the field, leaving the horse to wander happily around to his heart's content.

Clarrie charged into the farmyard. "Grandpa, Grandpa, come quick"

The old man was mending one of the stable doors. What was wrong with the boy now? Couldn't he manage a simple task like ploughing a field. Grandpa came out of the stable to find Clarrie rushing about the yard like a man possessed. "Well, what's the matter boy?"

"There are two Germans in the bottom field. They say they are going to build a bunker."

Grandpa looked puzzled. "What do they want to store coal down there for?"

Clarrie put on a superior look and sighed. "Don't be silly Grandpa. A bunker is where they put their guns to fire out to sea."

The old man had heard the Germans were building these funny concrete boxes all over the island but couldn't believe they were going to build one in his field. Maybe his grandson was having a joke with him. No, one look at the boy was enough to tell him this was no joke. There was definitely something going on in the bottom field that needed looking into.

"Right calm down boy, tell me exactly what you've seen."

Clarrie quickly told the old man the story, making it sound as if he had told the Germans a thing or two in no uncertain terms. Edmund Ahier slowly digested the full facts of this new intrusion on his property. His face turned red with rage.

"A lump of concrete in my field indeed. I'll soon sort them out."

He gave a violent spit, covering Clarrie's boots with tobacco juice. Then, leaving Clarrie staring at his boots, rushed off towards the bottom field.

For his age he was able to move extremely fast, even managing to pick up a large stick without faltering in his stride. The two dogs, sensing something was wrong, ran after him barking for all they were worth. The sight of Grandpa on the warpath was enough to frighten anyone, except of course Grandma, who could have stopped him with just one stare. The Germans heard the approaching farmer long before he came into their view. The sound made them look up to witness the sight of the old man rushing down the field waving a stick above his head and two fierce dogs barking at his heels. To the Germans he looked quite a comical figure. They glanced at each other, smiled, and shrugged their shoulders. Hooknose undid the clip on his holster and loosened his gun just in case of trouble.

The effort of running such a distance had taken its toll on the old man. He was starting to puff and wobble from side to side. It was the most strenuous exercise he'd had in months. On the other hand the dogs were thoroughly enjoying themselves. They hadn't had so much fun since Hedley had run over one of the chickens with his pushbike. On that occasion Grandma chased him round the fields for at least ten minutes, planting a painful kick on his backside every time the unfortunate Hedley had come within range. Grandpa was about ten feet from the Germans when one of the dogs, getting over excited, got tangled up in the old man's gumboots. Grandpa went crashing to the ground, rolled over, ending up in a heap on top of the dog. Hooknose suppressed his laughter, and reaching down, helped Grandpa to his feet. The old man straightened his hat, kicked the dog, who shot off up the field, then turned on the Germans.

"Get off my land and take your blasted lump of concrete with you."

Unfortunately, because he was so worked up, he had reverted to the local patois. The Germans didn't understand a word he said so they continued to calmly brush the ground off of his clothes. The old man, realizing his mistake, drew a deep breath and repeated his order in English. The German was firm but polite.

"I'm sorry but I'm just obeying my orders. Zey are to measure out and mark zee sight for a bunker to be built here."

By this time Clarrie had arrived on the scene with Grandma and Millie in tow. The sight of Grandma with her rolling pin in her hand, standing five foot ten and weighing sixteen stone did put fear into the Germans. They had never been instructed on how to deal with a situation like this. Millie wiggled her large hips and smiled at the Germans until Grandma noticed.

"Get back up to the house girl" then turning to her husband she withered him with one frosty look. "Leave this to me."

"Now" she demanded, with a force that made Hooknose take two steps backwards. "What's all this about?"

The German once again went through his explanation but this time he was more polite and apologetic.

"Rubbish. You'll do nothing of the sort. There's plenty of other places for you to go digging holes without coming here and mucking about on our property."

At that moment Hooknose was saved any further argument by the arrival of a German officer. He was relieved to see his officer for the first time in years as the Major was not a popular man. Major Frans Zimmerman had worked in a grocery shop before the war. He had the right connections so, when called into active service, he had started as an officer instead of in the ranks. He was a short thin man who, at first glance, seemed to be trying to re-create a portrait of Hitler. Black hair, heavily greased, was brushed straight down from the parting, and his dark complexion appeared to have a fixed glare. Not a man to be trusted. The soldiers joked that he would sell his own mother for a Reichmark. His small brown eyes seemed capable of staying open without ever needing to blink. He missed nothing and when angry, he would quiver like a jelly before exploding into an uncontrollable rage. On the few occasions his thin lips managed a smile, the flash of gold teeth would dazzle everyone in the radius of twenty feet. The Ahier's knew that this man was going to be a different proposition to Hooknose.

Major Frans Zimmerman climbed out of his car, glanced around at the gathering, then called Hooknose over to him. For a few moments they spoke in German with Hooknose pointing warily at Grandma with her rolling pin, and at the one remaining dog, who was still barring his teeth at everyone. The Major approached Grandma, and, completely ignoring Grandpa, started again with the same story. Because of his impeccable manners and thin, yet soft voice, Grandma was beginning to get flustered. Meanwhile Grandpa had calmed down and his brain was working overtime. As the officer turned to him he fell down on one knee and cried out. "Haro, Haro, Haro, a l'aide mon Prince, on me fait tort."

The German couldn't understand French so asked Grandpa to speak in English. The old man explained that in English it meant; "Haro, Haro, Haro, help me my Prince, I am being wronged."

He then proceeded to tell the German that the Clameur de Haro had been used in the islands since the days of Prince Rollo in the

11th century. Once the Clameur de Haro had been raised, the aggressor had to stop what he was doing and the point in issue would be taken to the courts for their decision. It had in fact been used at the funeral of William the Conqueror. As William was being buried, a certain Anselm Fitzarthur called out the Clameur de Haro. He was the owner of the plot of land being used for the burial and hadn't been consulted regarding the purchase of the ground. The funeral had to be halted whilst William's son bargained with the man until a price was agreed and paid in full. Only then was the funeral allowed to continue.

This baffled Major Zimmerman. He lit a cigarette and contemplated the situation. He was under orders to build bunkers but he was also instructed not to antagonize the locals. The Germans had allowed many of the local laws and customs to continue so in this instance he was undecided as to his correct course of action. He would have to refer the problem to his superior officer. He turned to Grandpa, clicked his heels, gave a slight bow and returned to his field car, taking the rest of the Germans with him. They drove off leaving Grandma waving her rolling pin at them. Millie, who had been watching everything from behind the hedge, just waved and smiled at the Germans. Grandpa climbed slowly to his feet, brushing off the remainder of the ground from his coat and trousers.

"That's got rid of them for a while although I don't think we've heard the last of this."

A few days later the Germans returned and started digging, but the bunker was built about twenty yards away from the original site, on a piece of waste land that didn't belong to the farm.

Grandpa smiled. Grandpa 1. Germany 0.

CHAPTER EIGHT

A Load of Bull

Grandpa was fuming. Those bloody Germans had been at it again. With autumn approaching the soldiers had resumed their football season, and the field reserved for the cows was the only flat patch of grass they had been able to find close to their bunker. The ball was constantly being kicked into the trees, therefore much of Grandpa's precious crop of cider apples lay on the ground. To add to his troubles, the Germans insisted on moving the cows to the top end of the field out of the way of the game. Therefore the grass in that area had been eaten so the milk yield was down. The time had come to pick the apples. Grandpa enlisted the help of all available hands on the farm, making every other chore wait until the crop of apples had been harvested.

"Tomorrow" he told the family. "We'll pick the apples and start making cider."

The Germans had long realized to their cost not to eat cider apples as they were bitter and caused dreadful stomach ache. Besides which, in exchange for a few cigarettes, Clarrie would supply them with a few bottles of the most beautiful farm cider. So the trees were left untouched, except of course, for the weekly football match.

The next day proved to be an ideal day for picking apples. A light breeze floated a few white clouds across an otherwise clear sky. Grandpa told everyone to make ready whilst he chained the cows out in the field. Clarrie went into the loft to fetch the baskets, whilst Hedley was sent to find the ladder. Grandma made pots of steaming coffee to fill the flasks so they wouldn't have to return to the house at break time. Meanwhile Millie was doing her face in the mirror, just in case any of the Germans saw her.

Grandpa came rushing back into the yard. He was cursing in local patois which usually meant trouble. He went straight through the yard towards a small patch of grass by the farmhouse. This was the private grazing area kept solely for the bull. Even though the bull was bad tempered and not to be trusted, he had learnt over the years to have a certain respect for the old man who was not in the least bit scared of him. Grandpa handled him as if he were a heifer and the bull was always meek when the old man moved him from one place to another.

Edmond Ahier pulled the chain out of the ground. "Right. we'll see what you're like as a centre forward my boy" He pulled the bull through the farmyard and off towards the field.

"Stop dawdling around Clarrie, follow me to the field bringing the ladder and baskets with you" he shouted over his shoulder.

The old man reached the gate, unhooked the bull from its chain, pushed him into the field, then gave him a kick up the backside which sent the bull charging down the field at a rate of knots.

The football match had only just started. The score was still level at nil-nil when the new centre forward joined the game. Hans was about to score the opening goal when he realized, by the expression on the goalkeeper's face, something was wrong. The sound of hoofbeats resounding in his ears made him swiftly glance around. He was greeted with the sight of the bull in full flight, making him forget completely about the goal. All hell broke loose. There were Germans running everywhere. Meanwhile the bull was having the time of his life. This was even more fun than when he had managed to get loose and wandered down the field where all those lovely cows were waiting for him. Grandpa had even been thoughtful enough to tie them down so they couldn't run away. He charged one way then another until every German was perched in an apple tree out of reach. He brushed against one of the trees, trying to dislodge a soldier but only managed to knock down a load of apples, one of them falling directly onto his head. The centre forward had most certainly won the day and it didn't look as if the game was over yet. They couldn't stay up there forever, so the bull stalked around, first going to one tree then another, staring up at each victim in turn, daring them to come down and start the second half. Ho, Ho, he thought, I'm the king of the castle and you're the dirty rascals.

Grandpa came slowly through the gate. He was pushing a handcart piled high with baskets. He hummed a little tune to himself as he pushed the cart down through the field. The bull sensed someone was approaching, turned, recognized his master and returned his attention to the Germans. They had also seen the old man and began pleading with him to chain the bull to enable them to climb down from the trees, but he didn't seem to hear them. He picked up one of the baskets and strolled over to the first tree.

"Hello, what are you doing up my apple tree?" The old man appeared to have been taken by surprise at finding a German up the tree. "You know you can't eat cider apples. Still whilst you're up there you may as well make yourself useful."

Edmond passed the soldier a basket telling him not to come down until the tree was stripped of apples. He then went around to the other trees passing a basket up to each German in turn with the same message. He then sat down under one of the trees and poured himself a cup of coffee out of the flask. The Germans looked at each other in bewilderment, not quite sure what to do. One by one they realized the old man had caught them. It was either pick apples, remain up the trees, or face the bull. Soon baskets of apples were being passed down from the trees to Grandpa who emptied them into the barrels then handed them back.

"Make sure you don't leave any. I want every single apple picked off those trees before you come down."

The rest of the family were watching from the safety of the hedge. The bull was docile with Grandpa but he couldn't be trusted near anyone else. So the game continued, the Germans picking apples, Grandpa taking the baskets off them, the barrels starting to fill with the precious crop, and the bull strutting about like the foreman of a gang of workers.

Now in every army there is always one officer who has the knack of turning up at the wrong moment. Major Frans Zimmerman drove around the bend in the track leading to the bunker. He felt at peace with the world. He wasn't in his usual bad temper, having just received a letter from home saying his mother-in-law had passed away. The family shop, which she had run for years, had been left to his wife. When he could finally return to Germany after this cursed war was over, he would be a rich man. He pulled up outside the bunker, climbed out of the car and was surprised to find no-one on guard duty. Assuming they were all inside having coffee he went to join them. A few moments later he emerged from the bunker a changed man. Where were those bloody soldiers? He was always having trouble with this group of men. It was time they were sent to the Russian front, that would wake them up. Looking around he noticed movement amongst the apple trees in a nearby field. The farmer must be picking his apples. Then he realized the people up the trees were wearing German uniforms. So his soldiers were stealing the farmer's apples instead of being on duty in the bunker looking out for enemy planes. He would sort them out once and for all. He marched through a gap in the hedge and strode up to the nearest tree.

"Hans, come down from zere immediately."

Ho, Ho, thought the bull. The second half is about to start. Grandpa, who had also seen the German officer, tried to reach the bull but was about two seconds too late. The bull tossed his head in the air and charged. Hans shouted, the officer turned, the bull hit the tree, once again two seconds too late. Major Zimmerman looked down from his perch at the bull, then up at the soldier who was sharing his tree.

"Vat zee hell is going on here?

Before he could get an answer from the soldier, Grandpa appeared at the foot of the tree, grabbed the bull by the horns and put the chain through the link in his nose.

"I'm sorry sir if the bull frightened you. He just got loose and came into the field. I've got him now so you're quite safe to come down. By the way, thank you for allowing your men to help pick my apples. They have been a great assistance. It would have taken ages to do the job by myself."

The old man slowly led the bull away. "Full time whistle has been blown old boy. Never mind, I thought you did well, played a good clean game and most certainly came out the winner."

The Germans came down from the trees. They sheepishly looked at the officer who, in his haste to get up the tree, had ripped his uniform. He was not a happy man. He pointed towards the bunker and the men trooped off in single file.

My, my, thought Grandpa. They didn't even shake hands at the end of the game or want to exchange shirts. What bad sports. Still that's the Germans for you. If you don't let them win they don't want to know you.

"Clarrie, collect the barrels and bring them up to the yard. I think you'll find all the trees have been stripped but check just in case. I'm going to give the bull an extra feed. I think he deserves it."

CHAPTER NINE

Grandpa 2 – Germany 0

The Germans on guard in the bunker, situated between the cliff top and the bottom field, gave Grandpa many headaches. They found him amusing, constantly thinking of pranks to play on the old man. They would climb over the hedge at night helping themselves to whatever was growing in the field at the time. In fact they were a thorn in the old man's side. At least once a week something would happen to send him rushing down the field to have a blazing row with them. Because of his age he was allowed to speak his mind to the Germans. Most of the time they had asked for it anyway. Gradually he began to know one or two of them by name and sometimes, without thinking, he found himself saying good morning when he passed them during the course of his work. On these occasions he hurried away to hide his embarrassment at having to admit he had grown to like a couple of them. Hans especially, was a nice lad. He came from a farming family and, on a few occasions, helped the old man with one or two little jobs, like mending the plough, when Grandpa had thought it was beyond repair. Then there was Gunter who kept showing him photos of his family back in Germany. Grandpa supposed if the lad had been given the choice he would have preferred to be at home instead of sitting on the edge of a cliff in some strange island. Still they had no right to be there and the sooner they were thrown out the better. The States didn't seem to be doing much about it and the local police were useless in controlling the looting of his crops.

Towards the end of October the Germans thought up a new trick to play on Grandpa. It was Clarrie's fault really. He had told them about Guy Fawkes day, what it meant and how it was celebrated. The Germans thought it was a good idea. They wished someone would do it again with the present English parliament, this time making a better job of it.

They pumped Clarrie for more information on the subject then, at night whilst they were on guard at the bunker, they formulated an idea. They decided to build a "Guy" resembling Grandpa, and then, on the appropriate day, burn it in full view of him. The framework for the "Guy" would be quite easy as there was plenty of timber lying around and they had all the nessessary tools. The problem was how could they make it enough like the old man for him to realize who it was supposed to be. One of them had done some art work at school so felt competent enough to be able to mould a face and paint it to resemble Grandpa. All the Germans by now called the old man Grandpa, a fact in itself which didn't go down well. Grandma, on the other hand, was still known as Mrs. Ahier. She had no sense of humour at all. The Germans were afraid of her and her rolling pin which she always carried whenever she had to visit the bottom field. After all, one of those nasty men might take a fancy to her, try and drag her behind the hedge, then have his wicked way with her. She had been brought up to believe any man in uniform had only one thing on his mind as far as women were concerned. The Germans had also realized that in any of their pranks, Clarrie would be a willing partner. They decided on this occasion he would come in useful as far as clothes were concerned. When approached it took all of five minutes before they could stop him from laughing. Soon a bargain was reached, three packets of cigarettes for some of Grandpa's old clothes.

During the next few days the Germans were busy. Some of them could be seen nailing pieces of wood together, others gathering leaves and other suitable material for stuffing the clothes with. One guard spent most of his time with a large piece of wood and a sharp knife, chipping gently away until a face started to appear. Things were progressing well. The Germans could hardly wait to stand the finished "Guy" outside the bunker in full view of Grandpa. They had to be extremely careful because their commanding officer, who was prone to make spot checks, like Grandma, didn't have a sense of humour so a careful lookout was kept for his approach. In fact they spent more time looking out for him than for enemy planes. Clarrie kept his part of the bargain well, producing some of Grandpa's old clothes that had been mended so many times Grandma had refused to mend them anymore, telling Clarrie to throw them away. Usually when she asked him to do something for her it took ages, this time, immediately upon her request, the clothes disappeared. Grandpa spent half an hour searching for them the next day giving up when his wife stated she had torn the clothes up for rags because that was all they were fit for. He didn't like it but knew better than to argue with her. So the Germans had everything they needed for their prank and Clarrie had three more packets of cigarettes for his store.

On the morning of the third of November the Germans came out of their bunker carrying their "Guy". They had decided to show him off for a while before burning him on the fifth. Smiling all over their faces they placed him near the top of the cliffs. The "Guy" could help them look out for enemy planes. Grandpa had been working in the bottom field for the last few days so they all waited outside the bunker for him to appear. It was a misty morning but once the mist cleared it promised to be a lovely day. Clarrie knew the "Guy" was ready so made himself scarce. His grandfather would eventually work out who the culprit was behind the disappearance of the clothes and come looking for him. As the mist started to clear Grandpa was sighted coming down the field. At the same time the drone of a plane could be heard somewhere overhead. The Germans hurried into their positions, trying to see through the morning mist in an attempt to spot the plane. They were too pre-occupied to hear the car pull up in the small lane alongside the field. Major Zimmermen jumped out and ran towards the bunker. He had also heard the plane, his eyes joined the search of the skies for a sign of the aircrafts markings. This battery had yet to see action. It would be a feather in his cap if this was an enemy plane and they could shoot it down. As he passed by the hedge he noticed Grandpa, also staring up to the sky.

"Morgan Mr. Ahier. Curse your mist, vhy is it alvays like zis over here?"

"To stop you from seeing our planes"

The Major ignored the old man. He would never grow accustomed to dealing with these locals. He knew his men played tricks on the old man and, whilst it didn't interfere with their work, he had turned a blind eye. He was still smarting from the last incident with the bull. He was just about to enter the bunker when he saw a figure standing near the cliff top.

"Hans, is zat you?"

No reply.

"Halt, who goes zere, stop or I vill shoot"

The figure didn't move. It was not a German soldier. As he moved closer he could make out the figure of an old man dressed in farmers clothes. Funny, there should be no other farmer around here, he thought. He had just said good morning to Mr. Ahier so it wasn't him. Major Zimmerman drew his gun and shouted. "Come over here, let me see your face"

The figure still didn't move. The Major fired a warning shot over the head of the intruder. This brought an immediate response from the bunker. The German soldiers charged out, guns at the ready. The sight of their officer firing at their "Guy" stopped them in their tracks. They didn't know whether to laugh or cry. The Major spun round as he heard them come out of the bunker.

"Arrest zat man"

The men looked at each other, uncertain as to their course of action they remained immobilized to the spot.

"Has everyvone gone deaf around here zis morning? First zis farmer, now my own men"

Just then a break in the mist showed a British plane flying low over the sea.

"Everyone back into zee bunker, bring zat plane down"

The Major forgot all about the farmer and rushed into the bunker to command his men. Grandpa was also too busy watching the plane to worry about the silent intruder who didn't seem to want to move for anyone. The plane was in trouble or it wouldn't have been flying that low. The gun opened fire and explosive sounds filled the air. Being the men's first action probably had something to do with the standard of their marksmanship. They blasted away without any luck for at least five minutes after the plane disappeared from view. Well done, thought Grandpa, another young pilot lives to return and fight the Germans.

When the firing finally stopped the Germans came out of the bunker. Major Zimmerman was not happy. These bungling fools had ruined his chance of glory. He gave his men a stiff lecture. Although Grandpa couldn't understand a word, he felt certain that compliments were not being passed to the gunners. The mist had suddenly lifted. Grandpa could now see the silent intruder quite clearly. So, the soldiers had made a "Guy" to look like him, even using his old clothes he had been hunting for. The old man spat out a mouthful of tobacco. They had gone too far this time.

Major Zimmerman finished the dressing down of his men. He was just about to return to his car when Grandpa called out a warning.

"Look out behind you, he's got a gun"

Frans Zimmerman suddenly remembered the silent man and spun round firing from the hip. Three bullets thudded into the "Guy's" chest. Still he didn't move. The Major stared. He couldn't possibly have missed, not at that range. Slowly the realization of the exact identity of his target made the Major go white with rage. He turned to Mr. Ahier who had shouted the warning. The old man was leaning against the hedge with a broad smile on his face.

"Your men made a good job of him, didn't they?"

Major Zimmerman looked back at the soldiers. Their faces gave them away. They had been up to their pranks again, only this time they had made him look stupid in front of the farmer. He ordered them back inside. Grandpa wished he could be a fly on the wall inside the bunker. After five minutes Major Zimmerman reappeared, his face red from shouting. He noticed Mr. Ahier was working near the hedge, still with a smile on his face. Frans Zimmerman turned quickly and strode to his car where the driver was trying hard to keep a straight face.

"Back to town as fast as you can drive"

The Germans came slowly out of the bunker. There was a frosty silence. None of them looked at the old man. They went up to the "Guy", pulled it out of the ground, and threw it over the cliffs then shuffled back into the bunker. Grandpa watched them silently. This prank had gone too far and he was determined to have his revenge.

Clarrie expected to be hauled over the coals that night but Grandpa hadn't said a word to anyone. He just sat by the fire all evening brooding and constantly chewing on his tobacco. Grandma inquired what was wrong but the old man ignored her and continued to stare into the fire. His grandson, who he would deal with later, had obviously supplied the clothes. Appropriate punishment for Clarrie could wait, the Germans had to be taught an immediate lesson. Because of the curfew, all lights had to be out by nine o'clock so everyone was used to going to bed early. That night Grandpa remained downstairs, saying he would wait for the fire to die down before he retired. After all, he could do his thinking just as well by the light of the fire and even better without the continual clicking of Grandma's knitting needles. It took an hour before a smile slowly spread over his face and he started chuckling to himself.

Grandpa rose early the next morning sending Clarrie down to the bottom field to finish off the work.

"I've more important chores to do here son" The old man had a glint in his eye that was making everyone nervous. Clarrie reached the bottom field to discover the Germans were not in a friendly mood. They hardly spoke and when questioned as to the previous day's activities, they turned their backs on him and went into the bunker. All day Grandpa was busy in his shed. The sound of hammering could be heard and he was asking for some strange things. Grandma's inquisitive nature couldn't stand the strain any longer. Taking him some coffee as a pretext, she tried to discover what he was up to.

"What on earth are you doing with all that wood and clothing?"

Don't bother me now, I'm far too busy. Do you remember where I put the remainder of the black paint I used on the old range?"

Grandma turned her back on him. He wasn't going to speak to her in that manner. She was more annoyed by the fact that, not only couldn't she understand what he was doing, he wouldn't tell her.

The old man worked non-stop, not even coming in for his dinner. Grandma made a rabbit stew especially for him but Clarrie saw it wasn't wasted.

"I don't know what he's up to. He's been asking for some strange things" "My scissors have gone, along with all the paper I was saving for the fire"

That night Grandpa sat by the fire again, only this evening a smile lit up his face. Clarrie was nervous. He knew his grandfather was up to something. He tried to go into the shed to have a look but the old man had locked the door for the first time in years. Grandpa retired early. As he was leaving the room he turned to Clarrie.

"In the morning gather all the scraps of wood and rubbish from around the place, cart them down to the bottom field and make a bonfire"

"You can't light a fire down there. Why not have one near the house where the Germans won't be able to see?"

"I want it in the bottom field son, as close as possible to the hedge without setting it alight"

The old man went to bed leaving the rest of the family scratching their heads, wondering just what the old fool was up to.

The next morning, the 5th of November, Grandpa disappeared into the shed once again after making sure his grandson had not forgotten to build the bonfire. Clarrie gathered all the rubbish he could find. There wasn't much because, under the hardships of the occupation, most things were utilized rather than thrown away. After about half an hour of hunting around he came up with enough for a small bonfire. The Germans were puzzled by the goings on but remained silent, enabling Clarrie to get on with his work as quickly as he could. Get it over with, he thought, then I might find out what he's up to. By noon the fire was ready. Clarrie went up to the farmyard to find his grandfather. The old man was having coffee when Clarrie reported his task was completed. Grandpa smiled and walked towards the shed.

"Stay indoors all of you and keep out of my way. On no account go anywhere near the bottom field for the rest of the day"

It was a clear bright day and the Germans were taking it easy around the bunker. The sight of Grandpa coming down the field carrying something over his shoulder caught their attention.

"Vat's he doing Hans? He should know better zan to light a fire here"

They watched as the old man came down towards the bonfire. One of them focused his glasses on Grandpa.

"Mien Got. Zee old fool has gone completely mad"

The old man straightened up. He made certain all the Germans were watching as he placed his "Guy" on the bonfire. The Germans were speechless. Standing in the middle of the small bonfire was a "Guy" that bore a marked likeness to Adolf Hitler. Black coat, armbands with the swastika painted on, and a peaked cap. Even the face looked like Hitler. The Germans could do nothing but stare as the old man made sure it was standing upright in the fire.

Fate often plays her hand at the wrong moment. The field car of Major Zimmerman suddenly appeared round the corner of the lane. When their officer saw what was happening in the field there would be real trouble. Grandpa saw the car pull up and was in two minds whether to continue his task or throw the "Guy" down, hoping the officer wouldn't see it. Major Zimmerman looked out over the sea then marched towards his men. They seemed to be ignoring him, instead they were staring over the hedge into the field. He turned to see what was holding their attention. His mouth dropped open and his monocle, to which he had not yet grown accustomed, fell to the ground.

"Stop. I'll have you shot if you light zat fire"

He climbed over the hedge and marched up to the bonfire. Grandpa had done his work well. It really did look like Hitler. Major Frans Zimmerman stopped in front of the fire and stared at the "Guy'. He had known the old man would retaliate in some way for his soldiers tomfoolery, but this he hadn't expected. The German took out a cigarette and thought for a few moments. The smoke curled up into the clean air. Grandpa silently stared at the German wondering what the Major was thinking.

"Clearing up some of your rubbish I zee?"

"Yes sir. it was starting to clutter up the place"

"But you know zat you can't go around lighting bonfires just ven and vere you like"

"Yes sir"

Major Zimmerman flicked his cigarette butt into the fire.

"If you light zis fire I vill have to arrest you"

The smouldering butt started to catch on the dry timber.

"Zen you had better go home and leave it"

"Yes sir"

The flames were now starting to appear at the base of the fire.

"Good morgan" The Major turned on his heels and made his way back to his car.

"Corbiere, as quick as you can, and vipe zat look off your face"

The flames were now catching Hitler's coat alight, a sight which kept the soldiers mesmerized. Grandpa looked at the "Guy", now well ablaze, and wondered what Clarrie would say when he found out Hitler was wearing his favourite trousers.

Grandpa smiled. Grandpa 2. Germany 0.

Clarrie gets into Trouble

Clarrie seemed to have the knack of landing himself in trouble with the Germans. Being caught out after curfew had become a regular occurence. He had been threatened with prison if he continued to disregard rules and regulations. He would already have been in prison except he was needed on the farm to help provide the Germans with the required crops and milk which they regularly commandeered. He knew one day he would push his luck too far, but his reckless spirit couldn't be subdued, consequently he continued to ignore the laws of the occupying army.

Clarrie checked the tides. If he arrived at the tower about 4.30. in the morning he would be able to fish for three hours and return just before dawn. The sun wouldn't rise until about 7.45. He figured he could be off the beach and on the road home by then. Grandpa enjoyed a piece of rock fish and as it was his birthday tomorrow, Clarrie thought it would make a good present. He found his net in the loft and bribed Hedley with a bottle of beer for the loan of his bike. He was ready. All he needed was a cloudy night, a few short sighted Germans, and they would all be eating fish for Grandpa's birthday.

The moon was hidden by a bank of thick cloud and a slight drizzle made Clarrie feel safe. The journey from the farm to La Rocco Tower, which is situated in the middle of St. Ouen's bay, had been uneventful. The German guards felt relaxed. Only a mad man would be out on a night like this or, of course, a man with his eyes on a fish supper. Clarrie hid the bike behind a hedge then made his way down to the beach. His timing was accurate as he just made the tower before the incoming tide cut him off from the shore. Once round the back of the tower he would be out of sight of any German lookout. He clambered down the rocks, edging as close as possible to the water. Pushing his net, on its long handle, around the rocks he was soon rewarded with a few small rock fish. By the time the first grey streaks of dawn were evident in the heavy sky, his catch had grown to over two dozen. Grandpa would be pleased. The old man might even open his brandy bottle and allow Clarrie a tot. He was so mean with his brandy he would still have some left even if the occupation lasted another fifty years.

The tide had now receded enough to allow him to return up the beach. Packing up his net and placing the fish in his bag, Clarrie made his way back up the rocks. Something whistled over his head, landing in the water behind him. A loud explosion followed, causing a spout of water to rise into the air. The noise was repeated, this time the shell landing amongst the rocks at the foot of the tower. Rocks hurtled up everywhere forcing Clarrie to fall flat on his face in sheer terror. He was too young to die, he still had plenty of good years ahead of him. Then there was the girl he had arranged to meet that night. What would she do if he was killed? She had been waiting her turn for over two weeks now. Clarrie's brain was in a turmoil. How could he get out of this mess?

The gunner pushed another shell into the breech. The last effort had been closer to the target. He adjusted the sights. He must make certain this time. He had been under fire himself from his commanding officer about his accuracy. Still, practice makes perfect and that morning had been designated for firing practice on La Rocco Tower. He lined the gun up, checking his calculations. This time everything seemed to be alright. The officer watched through his field glasses as the gunner prepared to fire. His warning shout cut through the morning air like a knife. The gunners finger froze on the trigger. A white flag was flying from the tower. Who the hell was out there at this time of day? They must have unwittingly surprised a commando raid. The soldiers rushed out of the bunker, leapt over the sea wall and ran down the beach.

Clarrie stood on the wall of the tower, his shirt tied to the pole of his fishing net. Surely they would see him and stop firing. He could see a dozen soldiers running down the beach towards him, guns at the ready. Thank God. He was saved.

The Germans were rather taken back to discover the commando raid was only one young local boy, his shirt tied to a pole, holding a large bag of fish.

"Vot are you doing here? Zis place is out of bounds"

Clarrie explained about his grandfather's love of fish and that as it was his birthday he had tried to catch some as a surprise.

"You seem to have done vell. Bring zem over here"

Most of the Germans, who had been on duty all night, were looking forward to their breakfast. The sight of so many fish cheered them up. They sent Clarrie to fetch some wood, then set about building a fire.

"What about my grandfather? asked Clarrie, as he saw all his precious fish going on the fire.

"Vish him happy birzday from us. You are lucky vee did not shoot you. You chose zee only gunner in zee German army who cannot hit a barn door at ten feet"

The gunner turned bright red and glared at Clarrie. "I vas close viz zee last shot" he pointed out.

Too bloody close, thought Clarrie, but he knew this was one time to keep his mouth shut. These Germans didn't seem quite as friendly as the ones who occupied the bunker at the bottom of their field.

"Vee must report your activities to our commanding officer so I vill require your name and address" the officer pulled out his grubby notebook and searched for a pencil. Clarrie gave him the details in an apologetic voice, then asked if he might go.

"Do not let us find you around here again during curfew hours. You might not get off so lightly next time"

Clarrie nodded, made his way over to his bike and peddled off down the road as fast as he could.

Grandpa was furious. "You've been out half the night, arrive back at some unearthly hour, the cows haven't been milked and all you can do is sit there and yawn"

Clarrie explained his reasons for being out late, ending with, "Happy birthday Grandpa"

"Happy birthday indeed. Doing your work properly and on time would be a good present"

The old man turned and stalked off towards his barn. He felt he had to tell Clarrie off but had a strange warm feeling inside knowing his grandson had bothered to take such a risk just to give him a birthday present. He would make it up to him by allowing him to have a small tot of brandy that night.

Clarrie worked hard during the day to catch up on the jobs he should have started earlier in the morning. He put the nights adventure to the back of his mind and buckled down to his chores. Around mid-day Hedley appeared in the field to summons him to the farmhouse where a German wanted to see him. Oh shit, thought Clarrie, now what are they going to do? The officer gave Clarrie a good telling off, reminding him that if he wasn't so necessary on the farm he would be sent to prison for breaking the curfew.

"Instead you vill report tonight to zee parish hall and stand on guard duty all night. Vee had some telephone lines cut last evening so you, and a few other offenders, vill vatch over zee hall and surrounding lanes to make certain it doesn't happen again"

Clarrie was not amused. There goes my date, he thought. He didn't fancy the idea of spending another night without sleep, especially when it meant standing around in the cold for twelve hours. Still, things could have turned out worse. He went back to work trying to think of a way round this latest problem. He must find some way of occupying his mind during the long night ahead. Of course, he smiled to himself, why not kill two birds with one stone. It was an ideal opportunity to have a night out on the tiles and keep the young lady satisfied.

After Grandpa's birthday tea, which had been washed down with a small tot of brandy, Clarrie just had enough time for a quick visit to the local. Here he was able to make the final arrangements for his night of pleasure. The young lady had been a bit hesitant at first, but Clarrie persuaded her that nothing could go wrong and she would be quite safe. He also added if she wasn't prepared to take the risk he knew of a few who would. This settled it, with the time and place fixed, Clarrie set off to report to a corporal at the parish hall who would show him the area he had to patrol. As luck would have it, the corporal turned out to be the same man who had accompanied the vet to the farmhouse. Clarrie had caught him with his trousers down in the kitchen after he had lost an argument with the dogs. He remembered Clarrie and made it quite clear he was going to enjoy giving Clarrie the worst area to patrol.

"You should get nice and vet here. You vill regret zee day you laughed at me for having my trousers off"

"Don't I get a gun? They might be armed and hurt me"

"If zey don't zen I vill" The German advanced on Clarrie.

He raised his rifle as if to hit him. As Clarrie winced, the corporal laughed. "Vee vill see if your sense of humour is still as quick in zee morning"

He turned and marched off down the road leaving Clarrie to patrol the long narrow lane. The rain had just started, making it an uncomfortable job walking up and down his beat. Clarrie wondered what he would do if he saw anyone cutting telephone wires. Probably help them, he thought.

Time seemed to drag by. Clarrie kept looking at his watch. At last the hands showed 11.15. He climbed over the hedge and made his way to a small barn where he knew it would be dry. He pushed open the door and threw himself down on the hay. After ten minutes had passed the door slowly opened and a voice called out, "Clarrie, are you there?"

"Over here my love. Come and make yourself comfortable"

The girl came over and layed down beside him in the hay. Let the local lads cut the wires, he thought, I've got another kind of duty to perform.

Where the hell was that bloody farmer? The corporal strode up the lane once more, looking behind any hedge or tree that could possibly have hidden a man. The rain was sheeting down. The soldier wouldn't have blamed the farmer for taking refuge. No-one was going to come out on a night like this to cut wires so he had been instructed to send all the guards home. The others had already been sent back to their houses, but the corporal couldn't find the young farmer. He was getting wet and decided the man must have already given up and left. He noticed a barn at one end of a field. At least he would be dry in there. He pushed open the door and walked into the peace of the barn. The sound of someone giggling in the far corner made him stop and raise his rifle. He cautiously moved forward. The lines on his face creased into a smile at the sight that greeted him.

"Been caught wiz your trousers down, have you?"

Clarrie leapt off the young girl and stared at the soldier.

Oh hell, he thought, not you again. Can't you get lost somewhere?

"You may go home now. Zee orders have come through from headquarters".

Clarrie stood up and smiled at the German.

"Thank you, it has been a most pleasant evening. We must do it again sometime."

"Anytime you vish" replied the corporal. "No madam, you are out after curfew. You must remain here viz me until morning".

Clarrie looked at the half naked girl. Oh well, he thought, you win some, you lose some. He strolled out of the barn leaving the girl staring forlornly after him. He would have to remember to cross her name off his list.

– 1943 –
CHAPTER ELEVEN

The Plane

Everyone in the vicinity heard the crash. It had happened after curfew so all doors remained firmly shut. All that is except one. Grandpa was just dropping off to sleep in his favourite armchair when the house shook and the accompanying explosion caused the dogs to howl and throw themselves at the door in an effort to get out and investigate.

"If I'm not mistaken it sounds like an aircraft has crashed, and somewhere on our property" The old man looked at Clarrie. "Put the dogs in the back room and come with me"

"It's after curfew Grandpa"

"Never mind, if it's on our property I want to see what damage it's done"

The two men let themselves out of the kitchen door, passed through the farmyard and moved down the side of the hedge. They could hear excited raised voices in the next field.

"There's a plane crash-landed by the bunker" Clarrie whispered. "I wonder if it's theirs or ours?"

"Only one way to find out, let's have a look"

The old man climbed over the hedge and hurried across the field. The huge frame of the bomber was only a few yards from the bunker and the soldiers were too busy pulling the bodies of the crew clear of the wreckage to notice that two extra figures had joined their group.

"Another few yards and your lump of concrete would have been flattened" Grandpa remarked to the German soldier who was bending over the pilot.

"You must go back to zee house please. Zere vill be many soldiers here soon and you vill be shot if zey find you here" Hans looked frightened and his voice trembled slightly as he gazed down at the dead man lying at his feet.

"I just wanted to make certain no damage had been done to my property"

In the distance they could hear vehicles approaching fast.

"Go now please, before it is too late"

Grandpa tugged Clarrie's arm, dragging his eyes away from the dead pilot, and the two men moved swiftly across the field. As they scrambled over the hedge Clarrie caught his foot on something large and solid. A section of the plane must have fallen off just before impact and landed in the hedge. The two men pulled at the splinted metal, finally managing to haul it over into the next field. By this time a large group of soldiers had appeared at the bunker and the lights from the trucks showed up the huge bomber clearly.

"Well that's one question answered my boy. One of theirs"

"Just look at this section" Clarrie kicked the piece of metal. "We've got part of the tail with a lovely Swastika on it. No good to us, may as well leave it here. It's too heavy to carry anyway"

"Break off some branches and cover it" ordered Grandpa. "I'd rather they didn't find it just yet"

Clarrie stared at the old man. What was he up to? The tail section of a German bomber was no good to them. Grandpa was already collecting a few branches so Clarrie kept his questions till later and helped cover the twisted piece of metal as best they could without help of a light. Even when they had returned to the safety of the house the old man still wouldn't answer his questions.

"Just wait and see what tomorrow brings" was all he would say.

Clarrie couldn't sleep. Large lamps had been erected down by the bunker and the glow lit up his bedroom. Unfortunately he wasn't able to see down to the ground level of the bottom field therefore he had no idea what the Germans were doing. Maybe the plane was loaded with bombs and the soldiers were unloading the cargo before the whole area disappeared into a puff of smoke leaving only a huge crater where the farm used to be. Clarrie shuddered. He was too young to die. He pulled the covers over his head and tried counting sheep but as they jumped over the sty they kept turning into huge bombs.

For the first time in living memory Clarrie was first up. He had washed, shaved and was having his breakfast before anyone else had even thought about rising. Grandma couldn't believe her eyes.

"What's the matter with you? Have you been up all night?"

"Couldn't sleep Grandma. I think I'll go and put the cows out. It'll save Grandpa a job"

He shot out of the kitchen, leaving the old lady scratching her head in amazement. Clarrie ignored the cow shed and made straight for the bottom field. He reached the hedge and peered over. The plane was still there, with a handful of Germans finishing the unloading of the aircraft. The early morning sunlight reflected off the plane making Clarrie squint to obtain a clear view. A few minutes later he was running back towards the house. He'd seen all he needed to see to be first with the news.

"We were wrong Grandpa" Clarrie rushed into the kitchen. "It wasn't a German plane but one of ours. It looks like one of our brave crews didn't make it back home"

The old man smiled but said nothing. He finished his breakfast, took his old coat down from behind the door, then glanced at his grandson who was finding room for a second breakfast.

"Let's go and have a close look, shall we?"

The two men strolled down through the fields. The soldiers were working hard to clear the wreckage from around the main body of the plane. They stopped and looked towards their commanding officer as the two men approached.

"You are zee farmer?"

Grandpa nodded, his eyes taking in everything about the plane to give too much notice to the German.

"Vee vill be clearing the area soon. Our glorious Luftwaffe has accounted for another of your bombers. Soon zere vill be no British planes left in zee skies" The German spat out the last few words, turned and kicked the fuselage.

"Seems to be a few parts missing"

"Zey must have fallen into zee sea. Zat is where all your planes vill be soon" Haughty Harry was getting tired of these two locals.

"You must move away from here at once"

"Okay. When you remove the plane maybe you would like the piece which fell into the next field as well. It's strange though, that piece has German markings on and this plane looks as if it has just come off the British assembly line. Maybe two aircraft crashed and you've only found one?" The old man's eyes twinkled as he grinned at the German. "Also you'd better wipe the paint off your boot from where you just kicked that plane"

The German went white with rage. Perspiration appeared on his forehead and his mouth had suddenly gone dry. He looked down at the tell tale mark on his boot. The two locals had departed. One appeared to be laughing whilst the other was looking slightly puzzled. The German soldiers had stopped work. They had spent all night painting the plane with British markings to make the locals believe it was one of their planes which had been shot down. Now their officer had kicked the wet paint and these two locals had also found another part of the plane. Soon the news would be all over the island and their whole night's work had been in vain.

Grandpa pulled the branches off the piece of tail section which they had hurriedly hidden the previous night. His stupid grandson was still asking questions. Couldn't the boy see the obvious. He hurried back towards the house. The good news had to be circulated before the Germans had time to put over their version of the night's happenings.

CHAPTER TWELVE

Christmas Party

1943 was drawing to a close. The occupation had now lasted 3½ years with no sign of it coming to an end. Many essential commodities were running out though the local people had discovered ways of substituting various hitherto unused items to replace those no longer available. Tea and coffee had long been replaced by parsnips, sugarbeet, acorns, green pea pods, carrots, mangolds and bramble leaves. Each person used their own substitute, whichever was more abundant at the time. Though many processes including baking, shredding, grounding and roasting, most local tables were seldom short of hot beverages. Sugar beet was grown freely with the syrup being extracted to supplement the sugar ration. Sultanas and currants for cakes were substituted with either sugar beet, elderberries or grapes, cut up into small pieces and dried. Jelly was made from a special seaweed called Carrageen, which was bleached and dried. Salt was extracted from sea water. Special black butter nights, with the butter being made from apples, became popular on many farms. Tobacco was issued each week but only 1oz per person. The farmers took to growing their own tobacco whilst other smokers, who weren't fortunate enough to have a plot of land or garden, used cherry or sweet chestnut leaves, butterburr, coltsfoot or clover. With such a mixture of substitutes, the smell of cigarettes or pipe smoking took on a new aroma not always acceptable to the sensitive nose of a non-smoker.

One of the most ingenious substitutes was the use of potatoes for flour. This was a long and laborious process. The potatoes were washed in their jackets, then mashed in a tin bath. Water was added and the pulp placed into a sack, then squeezed. The dirty water remained in the bath whilst the sack became filled with the pulp of the potatoes. Many locals, not sure of the procedure, made the mistake of thinking the pulp was the flour. A great deal of home baking went amiss through this misunderstanding. The dirty water was to provide the flour. Once strained, a thick layer of black pulp would remain in the bottom of the bath. Clean water was then added and mixed in with the pulp. After being allowed to settle, the straining would be repeated until the remaining pulp was white. This was then layed out in the sun to dry and eventually produce potato flour.

With all these problems, to provide a good table at Christmas was becoming increasingly difficult. Grandma however, was determined to celebrate the festive season with a party to equal all parties. Living under the German occupation, it was impossible to foresee whether this would be the last Christmas they would be alive to celebrate. Grandma had therefore made up her mind to celebrate in style. She started planning months in advance by hoarding all the substitutes she could lay her hands on. Her larder was brimming with goodies by the time Christmas approached. She tackled Grandpa about a party. At first he wasn't keen, he felt it would involve too much time and hard work plus make a hole in his private stock of brandy, but when she continued nagging he reluctantly agreed. Once committed, he threw himself into the idea with boundless energy, coming up with many innovations Grandma hadn't thought of. The tree would present no problem. He knew just the branch to chop down, even though it wasn't spruce, it would suffice. Paperchains could be made during the long winter evenings along with other decorations the youngsters could think of. All kinds of scraps were used to make the decorations that would add colour to the Christmas party. Hedley was bemused by all these arrangements as he had never before witnessed Christmas being celebrated in this manner by the Ahier family. A branch of a tree was placed in the bell tower above the main house. In the old days the bell was used to summon the workers in for dinner. Grandma had no need of this because the smell of her cooking was sufficient to bring the men in from the fields. With the preparation of food and decorations well in hand, the thought of presents entered everyone's mind.

Grandma found this problem easy to solve. With the cold weather coming, she decided to make warm clothes for everyone. Grandpa and Clarrie would each receive a coat, made from an old blanket. Millie would get a new dress out of a pair of curtains, whilst Hedley was desperately in need of new socks. Grandma spent all her spare evenings knitting and sewing. She had plenty of old wool so she made gloves for everyone as well. As least her presents would be useful and most welcome. As for the others, thoughts of what their gifts could be, made for a certain amount of brain searching, in Hedley's case a difficult job. With little money in their pockets and the shops virtually out of stock, the problem was enormous.

In every country occupied by enemy forces there are always people who are prepared to make a profit out of the plight of their fellow men and Grandpa had one or two contacts in the ever increasing black market. With the few pounds he had saved, he was able to purchase certain luxuries the family hadn't enjoyed for a long time. He wrapped them carefully, hiding the parcels in the barn out of the way of prying eyes.

Clarrie thought of giving everyone a packet of cigarettes out of his vast stock but, as he was the only one who smoked, he decided it would be rather pointless.

Millie was busy sewing every night but no-one could work out what she was making. Small squares of material, in all colours and sizes, were being cut out of any odd scraps she could find.

Hedley was also being secretive. He wandered around the farm with a broad smile on his face, imitating the cat who had got the cream. He had obviously solved his present problem. Clarrie reckoned everyone would receive a packet of chewing gum from the half-witted farmhand.

Christmas Eve was party night. The gramophone played constantly. Everyone joined in the dancing and games. Grandma dragged Hedley around the kitchen in a bad imitation of a waltz, then had to sit down for half an hour to rest her feet as the poor man had spent more time on her toes than his own. A game of pass the parcel followed with Grandpa in charge of the music. He had wrapped the parcel placing forfeits intermittently amongst the wrappings. Clarrie had to sing a song whilst Grandma was asked to perform the can-can. Millie had the task of finding someone and identifying them after she had been blindfolded and spun round. This proved quite easy because she caught one of the dogs who had joined in the fun. Hedley's forfeit proved to be the best. He had to imitate a German soldier. His efforts were rewarded with hoots of laughter from the whole family. The party was in full swing when a sound from outside the back door made everyone freeze. Four voices, in close harmony, were singing "Silent Night" in German. Grandpa opened the door to reveal the Germans from the bunker standing outside in a group. The singing brought tears to Grandma's eyes. Even though they were the enemy, their lovely voices were doing full justice to the carol. As they finished Hans smiled at the family who by now had gathered in the doorway.

"Happy Christmas to you all. Vee bring gifts for you"

A lump appeared in Grandpa's throat. He was lost for words. The old man stood back to let the Germans in. It was the first time any of the soldiers from the bunker had come up to the farm let alone entered the house. The dogs were uncertain how to react so they stayed in the corner of the kitchen with their teeth barred. Clarrie, who was on good terms with the soldiers, was pleased to see them and offered a bottle of beer to each German. In return they produced two rabbits they had snared.

"Vee thought you might find some use for zeese"

Grandma walked over and took the rabbits, smiled at the soldiers, thanked them for their kindness and asked them to be seated. The ice was broken and the party could continue.

The Germans had also brought individual presents. Cuff links for Grandpa, cigarettes for Clarrie, nylons for Millie, chewing gum for Hedley, and a specially wrapped present for Grandma.

"Vee made it just for you madam. It has taken many hours of vork for Gunter"

Gunter shrugged his shoulders and his lean face creased into a smile.

"It vas easy really. I hope you vill like it"

Grandma unwrapped the parcel. It was about a foot long and round. The last piece of paper came off to reveal a new rolling pin.

"Vee thought you might have vorn out zee old vun by now"

Even Grandma saw the funny side to the present and waved it around, as if trying it for size and weight.

"This will come in handy. I seem to be using my rolling pin quite a lot these days"

Grandpa produced his brandy bottle and everyone raised their glasses in a toast.

"To zee end of zee var"

"To the defeat of Germany" replied Grandpa, in local patois.

Over breakfast the following morning everyone exchanged presents. The men were delighted with their new clothes. Hedley was over the moon with the two new tyres Clarrie had made for his bike out of an old piece of garden hose wrapped around some rope. The women were thrilled with the chocolates Grandpa had managed to buy on the black market and Millie produced her little squares of material which served as handkerchiefs. Everyone was speechless when Hedley distributed his presents. For years the man had kept a trunk under his bed. No-one had ever been allowed to look inside although Grandpa knew it contained all Hedley had been left by his parents when they died. He had sorted through his most precious belongings to find the most suitable gifts for what was now his family. A shirt for Clarrie, two ties for Grandpa, a pair of knitting needles for Grandma and a large straw hat with fruit on one side for Millie. She was so over-joyed with the gift, she gave Hedley a big kiss on the lips causing the poor man to wander round the house in a complete daze for the next hour.

No-one had been allowed to go into the stables since tea time the previous evening. According to local superstition, no farmer would enter his cowshed on Christmas Eve because on the stroke of midnight they believed the cows went down on their knees to pray, and any human who witnessed this act would be dead before the year was out. But now, with Christmas day breakfast over, work had to continue on the farm. Clarrie had the task of mucking out the stalls whilst Grandpa took the cows out into the field. The Germans saw him coming and waved. The old man returned their greeting. Major Zimmerman was also present at the bunker. Even he seemed to be in a good humour. He was handing round cigars to all the soldiers and graciously offered one to Grandpa. The old man accepted. Clarrie would be pleased with this gift. It would be most pleasant after dinner with a tot of brandy. The happy gathering was suddenly interrupted by shouts from the top of the field. Hedley was trying out his new tyres by cycling over the field. Grandpa looked again. What on earth was Grandma up to? With one hand lifting her skirt and the other wielding her new rolling pin, she was chasing after the unfortunate Hedley.

"Oh dear, it looks like he's forgotten to take his boots off before walking into the kitchen again"

Gunter laughed. "Either zat or she's testing her present"

"I hope she doesn't break it on his head. I've got a feeling she's going to need it before this war is over"

The Germans cheered as the two figures disappeared behind the hedge. Ploughed fields were not the easiest of places to ride a bike and Grandma was definitely gaining.

"So much for the time of peace and goodwill to all men"

"Goodvill to all men vizout muddy boots" replied Frans Zimmerman.

"Another veek and it vill be 1944. Zee var vill be over soon"

"I'll say Happy Christmas and goodbye now then"

He turned and strolled slowly back up the field. Better go and rescue Hedley before Grandma feeds him to the bull. He straightened his new tie. After all, Hedley wasn't a bad lad, just stupid.

He arrived back at the house to find Clarrie curled up with laughter.

"What's Hedley been up to now?"

Clarrie couldn't speak for laughing. He pointed towards Millie who was standing in the doorway looking out over the fields for a sign of a bicycle or a rolling pin.

"What on earth's been going on here?"

At that moment Hedley came into view. He was completely out of breath and ready to collapse. Grandpa caught his bike and stopped the chase going any further. Grandma came around the corner a few seconds later in much the same state as Hedley. She was so much out of breath, she didn't have enough energy to raise her rolling pin to strike him.

"Calm down everyone. Tell me what's going on?"

In between deep gulps of air Grandma pointed at the unfortunate man and demanded that he be driven away from the farm.

"He proposed marriage to Millie"

Grandpa turned slowly towards Hedley.

"You did what?" The old man stared at the youngster. It was so totally out of character he couldn't believe this squirming imbecile in front of him even knew what marriage meant. Then he remembered the kiss Millie had given Hedley after the presents had been given out. Grandpa began to comprehend the reason for the worm having turned.

"I think Millie brought it upon herself. Hedley was confused after the kiss she gave him" Grandpa felt an urgent need to calm matters down.

"Let's forget this incident and go inside for our dinner"

Grandma wasn't at all convinced, but it was Christmas, Millie had rather overdone the kiss, and Hedley was, after all, a bit simple.

"Just make certain he's never left alone with her again" Grandma placed her rolling pin down beside her plate.

"I'm going to keep this handy in future"

This is most certainly turning out to be an unusual Christmas thought Grandpa. First we get sung to by the Germans, then Hedley finds his manhood and proposes to Millie. Clarrie still laughing, turned to Hedley and with tongue-in-cheek said, "Hi, brother-in-law"

The old man could see the funny side of this new Hedley but at the same time knew things would never quite be the same again. The lad had grown up all of a sudden. He now knew the meaning of the strange feeling in his groin and was interested in using his new found knowledge. Maybe he wasn't as stupid as most people thought.

Grandpa raised his glass of cider. "Happy Christmas everyone"

CHAPTER THIRTEEN

Hedley Goes to War

Hedley couldn't seem to pull himself out of the daze Millie's kiss had left him in. He moped about the farm in a world of his own. Love had entered his small domain. Before, life had been uncomplicated, living one day to the next without a single care. A bed to sleep in, three square meals a day and a few shillings each week in exchange for his services on the farm. He was only asked to do menial jobs and at no time did he have to strain the grey cells in his brain or come up with any opinions of his own. Now everything had been turned upside down. Millie had given him the kiss of life. All because of his mother's old hat. The Ahiers wouldn't hear of him courting their grand-daughter, in fact Grandma had wanted him thrown off the farm for even thinking about it. Grandpa had understood, but was still firmly against the idea of having Hedley as one of the family. Clarrie thought it was funny and never stopped pulling his leg. Hedley didn't see anything amusing in the idea of wanting Millie. Clarrie wanted many girls but he only wanted one. He knew he didn't have much to offer but she was welcome to everything he owned. He decided he wouldn't be put off by the reception he had received after his first proposal, he would try and try again. The subject would demand a great deal of thought, something Hedley wasn't too good at. He would have to seek out someone who could give him some advice on the subject. Clarrie was no good. Firstly he wasn't married and therefore wouldn't know how to propose to a girl. Then of course he would just laugh at him and start calling him brother-in-law again. No, it had to be someone away from the farm. Someone who was married and could give him serious advice on how to go about courting Millie properly. He went about his work half-heartedly, his mind pre-occupied with more important matters.

Saturday night came round without any further developments. Hedley hadn't been able to come up with any bright ideas and his brow was becoming more crinkled every day as one thought after another was discarded as impracticable. He knew he would die for

Millie but would rather find a way to live with her. Millie, for her part, showed a certain amount of amusement at his advances. She had never thought of Hedley as a knight in shining armour, but in her position she couldn't afford to turn down any offer without giving it careful consideration. She couldn't really see herself married to Hedley. He was not only simple but he had no prospects and didn't even know what a bath was. She had to side with her grandparents on this issue. Hedley wouldn't do. The Saturday evening routine was always the same. The three men would go off to the local, leaving Grandma and Millie alone in the house. Grandma knew this would be the perfect opportunity to have a quiet word in her grand-daughter's ear. There must be no more encouragement for Hedley's advances. He was not suitable and never could be, so the matter must be settled once and for all. Grandma was firm but tried to be understanding at the same time. Her husband had pointed out to her, in strong terms, that she was responsible for much of what had happened, by the way she had kept Millie under wraps all these years. Grandma had given a great deal of thought to what her husband had said and decided the time had come for Millie to be allowed more freedom. She didn't want her grand-daughter to turn into an old maid. She just wanted the best for her and that didn't mean Hedley.

The three men sat quietly in the local. As Clarrie had predicted a few years previously, beer was in short supply. In fact it was so hard to come by that the most you could hope to find in the bar was watered down cider. Still, the social side remained, so all the farmers met each week in one corner of the pub to play cards and dominoes. Grandpa and Clarrie were busy around the card table so Hedley wandered up to the small bar. A group of young men were sitting in one corner chatting and laughing. He recognized one as Ted Carre's son. Now there was a man who could help him. Edwin Carre had recently got married so he must know the ropes. Hedley went across to the group and stood listening to their jokes. He found himself missing most of the punchlines but laughed when all the others laughed so his presence didn't stick out like a sore thumb. After twenty minutes the jokes started to die down and one of the young men went to the bar to refill the glasses. Hedley wasn't included in the round but that didn't worry him. He was already on his second half of cider which was his limit. He sat down alongside Edwin Carre who turned and smiled at Hedley.

"Could I have a word with you in private?" He didn't want the whole bar to know about his predicament.

"Sure. I'll just get my drink and meet you over by the bar"

Edwin had known Hedley all his life. The two men were about the same age and had grown up together. Even though Hedley was considered to be the village idiot he was a likeable idiot and all the young men of the parish were prepared to pass the time of day with him. The Carre farm was only a short distance from High View and the two farmers helped each other out when problems arose. If the Carre's needed a hand in an emergency, Hedley would be sent along to help. Ted Carre always seemed to be in trouble. His two farmhands had been English and were both deported to Germany soon after the occupation had started. Consequently Hedley spent many hours helping at Longfields, working alongside Edwin, especially at harvest time. In exchange Ted Carre would send down some of his modern machinery to help bring in the crop at High View. Hedley enjoyed working at Longfields because he didn't always get the blame when anything went wrong. Edwin used to keep him supplied with chewing gum during the working day and if they were inside the air wasn't constantly polluted by cigarette smoke as it was when he worked with Clarrie. Edwin was a bright lad. He knew how to mend the farm machinery when it broke down. He was even repairing an old motor car which was to have been dumped. When the occupation was over and petrol became available, he would be able to visit the capital city in his own motorized transport and be the envy of all the local youngsters. Edwin had always stood out above the rest. At school he always came top of the class. Poor Hedley had never been good at lessons and Edwin was the only boy who had offered to help. Now maybe he could help Hedley again with his urgent matrimonial problem.

"Well it's a personal matter. You see I want some advice from you on how to court a young lady"

Edwin smiled to himself. Something told him to check the laughter and his face remained serious. Even if the thought of Hedley wanting to court a young lady was funny, it obviously wasn't funny to the man himself. Love must come to everyone, even to people like Hedley.

"So you want to court a young lady? Who is the lucky girl?"

Hedley didn't know how to answer. He didn't want to disclose the name of his chosen bride.

"Never mind. We'll just call her Miss X. Now first of all you must smarten yourself up. I mean look at you. You've been wearing those same clothes ever since I can remember"

"I bought them ten years ago in a jumble sale"

"Yes, I know you did. They used to belong to me. But you've worn them ever since, haven't you? Your hair is a mess and when was the last time you had a bath or cleaned your teeth?"

"What's my hair or teeth got to do with courting a young lady?" he asked, after failing to come up with a suitable answer himself.

"A young lady goes by the appearance of the man who is trying to court her. She likes to see a smart presentable man calling at her door to introduce to her parents as her latest beau. You must take more pride in yourself my lad. Then you are half-way there. Also, when you talk to this young lady you must take that infernal chewing gum out of your mouth. No-one can understand a word you're saying half the time. Become smarter in your appearance and you could win your fair lady. Remember, you are out to impress the parents as well as your chosen girl. I must get back to the lads now but feel free to ask me any further advice later. Think on what I have told you, do something about it, and Miss X won't stand a chance. Just make certain I get an invite to the wedding"

Hedley thanked Edwin who moved back to the corner and told his mates about Hedley's problem. There was much laughter coming from the group of young men and smiling faces turned to look at the new Hedley. The question on everyone's lips was, who could the mysterious Miss X be? Hedley was deep in thought so he didn't notice the merriment he had caused in the bar. Curfew time was approaching so the pub closed and the men made their way back to their various farms. Hedley had been given food for thought and he sat up late in bed thinking about all the ideas Edwin had given him. He must do something about his appearance. He would start first thing in the morning.

Hedley woke early the next day. He had much to do before he went downstairs for his breakfast. The trunk came out from under his bed. Inside was all that was left of his parents belongings. He searched through the few possessions until he came across some of his fathers old clothes. He laid them out on the bed. Not quite the latest fashion but an improvement on his usual outfit. Hedley tried on a pair of trousers. They fitted him around the waist but his father had been a short man so the legs were not quite long enough. Still, a pair of boots would hide this defect. Next Hedley found a shirt. This had been his father's Sunday best so it had to be better than the one he already wore. He donned the new clothes and inspected himself in the mirror. How smart he looked. Millie would certainly notice him now. A few more additions from the trunk and he was ready. Wait, Edwin had also said something about his hair and teeth. Hedley went downstairs to the washroom and looked around. Soap was in short supply but Grandma had boiled some ivy leaves until soft, then added half a packet of soap powder and a tablet of soap, so increasing the quantity. Hedley spent ten minutes scrubbing himself. He also used the soap on his teeth ending up blowing masses of bubbles everywhere and feeling sick. This washing wasn't all fun. The water was cold and he was now shivering. He couldn't understand why anyone would want to go through this procedure every morning. He had no comb for his hair because he had never needed one before. He thought for a few moments then remembered the special curry comb he used on the horse. Using the side door he went across to the stable and borrowed the comb. He felt sure the horse wouldn't mind. It was all in a good cause. His hair was thick and curly so combing proved to be difficult. He had seen Clarrie comb his hair before going out on a date and tried copying the movements he made. Clarrie always used to wet his hair first so Hedley went outside and turned on the tap. Water gushed out over his head and splashed onto his new clothes but he was now able to pass the comb through his hair more freely. Clarrie had a parting in his hair so Hedley also decided to give himself one. Not certain just where the parting should go, Hedley chose the easiest method and parted it straight down the middle. He straightened his clothes, patted down his new hair style and made for the farmhouse. The smell of breakfast told him he was late so he hurried into the kitchen.

"Take off your boots and........." Grandma was lost for words.

Clarrie choked on a piece of toast. Grandpa stared at the apparition standing before him.

"What the hell.....?" Words failed him also.

Millie thought Hedley looked smart, a trifle overdressed possibly, but definitely smart. Pin-stripped trousers with the legs ending just below the knees, a white shirt and a green bow tie with yellow dots. Yes, a bit overdressed for a farmhand, but smart. Hedley looked pleased with himself. He smiled at everyone, bubbles still coming out of the corner of his mouth, and took his place at the table.

"You look different this morning" said Millie, placing his breakfast in front of him.

Clarrie choked on his coffee. Grandpa was still lost for words.

"Are you intending to work like that or is this some kind of fancy dress?" inquired Grandma.

"My new image. These clothes were my father's and as they're now mine I thought it was time I used them"

Grandpa found his voice, even though it was a little hoarse. "Let's see what they look like after you've mucked out the stables?"

Clarrie choked on his cigarette.

During the following week Hedley tried everything. He washed every day. Combed his hair until he thought it would all fall out. His teeth shone and he changed his shirt twice a week. After once a month this was a definite improvement. Millie still didn't fall for his charms. Grandma hadn't welcomed him with open arms and Clarrie was in grave danger of choking himself to death. Poor Hedley didn't know what to try next. He felt uncomfortable in these strange clothes and they made working on the farm difficult. The bow tie was hurting his neck and everytime he took off his boots he revealed the ridiculous length of his trousers. Something else had to be done, but what? He decided to tackle Edwin Carre on Saturday night and see if he could come up with a second plan of action. Surely there must be an easier way of courting a young lady than dressing up in unsuitable clothes and scrubbing your skin until it shone. There had to be another way.

The following Saturday evening Hedley cornered Edwin in the local. General laughter had greeted his arrival in the pub as he was still wearing his comical outfit although he was too pre-occupied to notice. He told Edwin of the goings on during the previous week and asked if he could suggest something else. Edwin smiled sympathetically at Hedley.

"We'll have to put plan two into action. You must prove yourself a man in her eyes"

"How can I do that?"

"Well now, if you were in uniform it would be easy. Girls go for men in uniform. As it is you'll have to think of some brave deed you can do to show Miss X you are a man"

Hedley sat in the bar and racked his brains. What could he do to prove himself a man? Learn to control the bull? No, that was too dangerous. Tackle Grandma and show her he was a man not a mouse. No, her rolling pin was always too handy and it hurt. Once again he sat up all night in bed trying to think of something he could do to prove himself. By dawn his brain hurt and he was too tired to think anymore. He couldn't even bother to wash or comb his hair. He just wanted to sleep.

It was Grandma who put the idea into his head. The Germans had issued a set of new rules that hadn't been too well received by the locals. Why can't someone make a stand against them, she had asked? Surely there's one man amongst the entire population who is prepared to stand up to this bullying hoard. Hedley stuck out his chest, causing a button to fall off his shirt. Yes, there was a man who was prepared to stand up to them. But how? It needed some meditation. That night he rummaged through the trunk under his bed. His father had been in the first world war and the trunk contained some of his relics and souvenirs. These may help. Now to formulate a plan of campaign against the Germans. One that would drive them away from the island for good. He would liberate Jersey and become a hero. Everyone would hail him as the conquerer of the German army and Millie would be his. Even Grandma would welcome him with open arms. He used all his spare time searching the farm for certain items he would need to help him conquer the innumerous Germans who occupied the island. This was going to be Hedley's finest hour.

The German officer arrived just as the family were sitting down to breakfast. No, Hedley was not with them. He must be washing or combing his hair in the stable.

"Nien. Zere is a man in Gronez Castle who has raised zee Union Jack. He fits zee description of zee man you call Hedley. My men vould have shot him but von of zem recognized him and has told me he is simple and lives viz you. I have come to ask if you can talk him out of zee castle before my men use him as target practice"

Grandpa shook his head. What was the idiot up to now?

Clarrie choked on a piece of toast.

Gronez Castle was built around 1328 on Jersey's northwesterly point as a refuge from the French. It had been captured in 1468 and left in ruins. Little of the fortifications remained and Hedley couldn't have chosen a more desolate spot to make his stand against the Germans. The perimeter of the castle was approximately 250 yards long and only the remains of the front battlements were left standing. There had once been a gatehouse and drawbridge over the moat, with two bastions, one on each side, which had six foot thick walls with arrow slits to enable the archers to fire down on the foe beneath. The whole building had been covered with a battlement roof which had long disappeared. All that remained was a pile of rubble and stone. Here Hedley had decided to make his stand and fight for his manhood.

The Ahier family accompanied the German the short distance from the farm to the castle. Above the remains of the main gate flew the Union Jack. The man had gone mad. Grandpa was certain of that.

"Vee do not know if he is armed. He hasn't fired on us and vee haven't fired at him. Vill you please see if you can get him out of zere before my commanding officer hears of zis. Vee understand zat he is simple and zat you are in charge of him so vee vill leave it to you to end zis charade"

Grandpa marched up to the entrance of the castle. "Hedley, come out of there immediately"

A head, wearing one of Grandma's saucepans, popped up from behind the battlements. "Stay away Grandpa. I'm armed with a sling and plenty of stones. I'm going to kill the Germans just like David did to Goliath in the bible. The vicar told us about it the other week. Anything he can do I can do as well"

As if to confirm his words Hedley let loose a hail of stones which fell amongst the soldiers causing them to hurry for cover.

"Don't be stupid boy. Come on out now and nothing will happen to you. If you persist in your action then the Germans will open fire on you"

"I've got a bow and some arrows here as well. I'm going to liberate the island and become a hero"

Grandpa shook his head in disbelief. Clarrie choked on yet another cigarette. Millie decided it was all her fault so she tried to coax him out of the castle.

"Hedley. I think you are so brave to stand up to the Germans like this. I'll always look upon you as a hero in future but I think you should lay down your weapons and come home before your breakfast gets cold"

"Not until I've driven them off the island for good" came the reply.

The German officer was starting to lose patience with the proceedings.

"Either you get him down from zere quickly or I vill order my men to open fire"

Grandma stepped forward. "You men are pathetic. You allow one simple man to defy you with a few stones and a bow and arrow"

She pulled her rolling pin out of her coat pocket and advanced upon the castle. The German soldiers drew back as the old lady passed them. Hedley saw her coming and pleaded with her to remain where she was. Grandma was having nothing to do with his threats. She went through the entrance of the castle and marched up to the unfortunate man. One swift swipe with her rolling pin ended all combat. Hedley came running out of the castle hotly pursued by Grandma.

"You leave your breakfast go cold on the table, cause us all this trouble and pinch one of my best saucepans into the bargain" She planted a kick on his backside. "Hero indeed. Wait till I get you home, I'll soon sort you out"

Hedley rushed passed the soldiers. He was wearing his father's first world war uniform complete with medals. As with the rest of his father's clothes, the trouser legs were far too short. Also the green bow tie didn't match the rest of the outfit. The saucepan on his head finished off a comical sight which caused the Germans to collapse into fits of laughter. Grandpa shrugged his shoulders and followed his wife in pursuit of Hedley.

The German officer didn't report the incident. He felt it was best left to the Ahiers to dish out the punishment to their simple farmhand. Anyway it had been amusing and no harm had come to any of his men. Grandpa wasn't going to forget so easily. He had been made to look a fool in front of the Germans. His wife had been able to control Hedley where he had failed. He wasn't going to forgive and forget in a hurry. Hedley would be given all the dirty jobs on the farm for the next month and could go on short rations. Grandpa also decided to have a word with Edwin Carre next Saturday evening. Plus, if his grandson choked once more it would be for good. Hedley the hero had fought his last battle. Grandpa would see to that.

CHAPTER FOURTEEN

The Football Match

The arguments had been going on ever since the Germans had made the challenge. The Le Vivier family felt they should supply six players, with only five coming from the Robbidane family. The Robbidane's had a different view. They had six good players who were much better than any Le Vivier, so there was no doubt in their minds as to who should supply the larger number of players. A truce was finally made when old man Vibert from Le Coin Farm suggested that his son could play in goal to enable the two families to supply five players each. The Germans found the family feud mildly amusing. They felt it didn't matter who played, as their team was going to win anyway. After all, they spent two hours every week practising and their football team was ready to take on the whole of Jersey let alone the parish side of St. Ouen. These idiot farmers were no match for the well equipped and organized German team, the only problem was going to be keeping track of the number of goals they scored. The German goalkeeper had even asked for a chair so that he wouldn't get tired standing round all afternoon.

The Germans supplied a gallon of petrol to enable a farmer to cut the grass. Petrol was such a precious commodity that the farmer put his cows in to do the work and sold the petrol on the black market. The unfortunate result was a well cut football pitch littered with manure. The mole hills would also cause a problem to any player who wasn't looking where he was going. When he collected his cows, farmer Le Brocq removed a few of the protruding mounds of earth then gave it up as a bad job, realizing that there must be an army of moles at work underneath the pitch. The overworked secretary at the Parish Hall was ordered to find the nets which had disappeared the previous year. He had little success until an old fisherman came to his rescue and offered some ancient fishing nets. A few hasty repairs and the goals were rigged out as near perfect as possible.

Someone had even come up with a pot of paint and the local layabout, Shakey Sam, was hired to trace the necessary white lines.

He proved to be true to his name as the side lines were anything but straight and one of the penalty spots had even been painted outside the area. Nevertheless the meadow looked vaguely like a football pitch even down to dirty pieces of cloth tied to bamboo canes for corner posts. Everything was ready for the big match and many wagers were made as to the outcome, with the odds on favourite being an early and abrupt finish to the game on account of the five Le Vivier's and five Robbidane's who were supposed to play on the same side, falling out with each other.

No-one knew for certain when or how the feud between the two families had started. Even the many children and grandchildren on either side didn't really understand why they hated each other. It was just an inbred feeling and no meeting ever passed without either a verbal or physical confrontation. The idea of a football team comprising of five members of each family was enough to ensure that the small ground would be packed to capacity. The result of the game was immaterial, there was going to be fireworks for certain and everyone in the parish wanted to be a witness.

Sunday turned out to be a glorious September day. Before the occupation most families would have taken a picnic lunch and gone to the beach. During the last few years it would have been impossible to have filled a hamper with goodies. Food had become too scarce for picnics. Also a farmer worked seven days a week if he wanted to make a living from his few small fields. This Sunday was different. Hardly anyone in the parish had spoken or thought about any other subject for the past week except the football match. Even the vicar had said a special prayer during the morning service for the local team. It appeared God had taken sides and with his help the local lads might even find the inspiration to beat the Germans.

Grandpa searched amongst his belongings and found an old rattle which he had used at a long forgotten Muratti. It seemed an age since Jersey had taken on Guernsey and Alderney in the Channel Islands football championship. He wondered if the islands would ever again play for the honour of holding the Muratti Vase aloft, and to receive the jubilant applause of their supporters. He also found a red and white scarf. The Jersey colours would do because he felt St. Ouen were representing the island when they took on the German Army. Clarrie decided to wear a red and white checked shirt although Grandma insisted on wearing her thick cardigan and woolly hat as she felt it might get cold standing around in that field. Hedley was true to form. He'd come straight from mucking out the cow shed and looked as though he'd slipped. There was a definite smell coming from his direction which caused him to be instructed to walk a few paces behind everyone else as the family made their way slowly to the field of battle. Millie had a cold so she stayed at home. Football was a stupid game anyhow. She couldn't understand how men could enjoy themselves chasing around after a piece of leather.

The entire population of the parish appeared to have turned out to witness the spectacle. Many were armed with hooters, rattles and whistles. Those who had been unable to find some form of musical instrument were carrying tin cans which made a frightful noise when everyone decided to show their enthusiasm at the same time. Behind one of the goals the Germans were assembled in full military uniform. They tried singing the German national anthem but every whistle, hooter, bell and tin can joined together to drown the singing completely. The cheers from behind one goal were drowned by whistles as the German side took to the field. They were smartly turned out in white shirts and black shorts and all had football boots which had been flown in from Paris just for the game. They made a great show of warming up, passing the ball from player to player before giving the goalkeeper some catching practice.

To wild applause the five Le Vivier's came onto the field. They had changed in the corner of the field occupied by the remainder of their family. The Robbidane's had chosen the opposite corner in which to change. Their family gave the five brothers a rapturous welcome as they ran onto the pitch. Each family had brought their own ball allowing both groups to warm up separately. Claude Vibert strolled onto the pitch from the halfway line. He knew better than to mix with either faction. To have changed with one of the families would have resulted in a good hiding from the opposite corner. He took his place between the posts and hoped someone might fire the odd shot at him. Whichever ball came his way he made certain it was thrown back to the right family. He was a survivor. This was one story he wanted to tell his grandchildren. Claude Vibert had a strange feeling he might start the match with five Le Viviers and five Robbidanes in front of him, but he wasn't certain how many would be there at the end.

The referee had been specially brought all the way from St. Helier. This would make certain he would favour neither side. His dislike of the country farmers would be as great as any animosity he felt towards the German troops. He had brought two players from the town football team to act as linesmen and complete the panel of impartial judges. The referee called for the two captains. This had caused a great deal of argument amongst the two local families until once again old man Vibert had come to the rescue and the St. Ouen's goalkeeper came forward for the tossing of the coin. He had been praying to lose, therefore enabling the Germans to have the choice of ends. This was due to the Le Viviers wanting to kick one way and the Robbidanes the other. God must have heard his prayers because the coin, which had been supplied by the German captain, came down heads, then seemed to magically disappear off the pitch. The Germans chose to play up the slope for the first half giving themselves the advantage of the wind whilst hoping the local side would run out of steam during the second half when they had to negotiate the steep slope. The two teams lined up, the referee checked his watch, gave a sharp blow on his whistle and the big match was under way.

The first half started off extremely scrappily with both teams finding difficulty in negotiating the bumpy pitch. The mole hills were making the passing of the ball along the ground almost impossible and the long high ball was catching the forwards constantly offside. The Germans were undoubtedly the stronger side and the ball was spending more time in the St. Ouen's half. Claude Vibert was playing a good game, executing numerous fine saves to the immense pleasure of the vast crowd of spectators. Frustration at the goal-less scoreline was beginning to show in the play of the Germans whilst the first signs of trouble between the two families was starting to rear its ugly head with the Le Viviers getting tired of the Robbidanes being constantly caught offside. It was one such offside incident which led to the opening goal. After some good defensive play the long ball out caught three Robbidanes well in front of the German defence. All the Le Viviers ran forward to remonstrate with the Robbidanes, leaving the St. Ouen half empty except for the goalkeeper. Whilst the families were locked in a fierce argument, the Germans took a quick free kick, and from inside their own half, mounted a one man attack to avoid being offside themselves. With only the goalkeeper to beat, the centre forward made no mistake despite a desperate attempt by Claude Vibert to rugby tackle him outside the box.

The goal brought jubilation to the Germans and was enough to light a match to the explosive undercurrent between the families. The soldiers watched in part amazement and part amusement as the brothers commenced a grand punch-up in the centre circle. All the bodies had to be separated, after which one Robbidane had to be carried off and one Le Vivier was sent off. St. Ouen was now one goal down and only nine men remained on the pitch. The families were now hurling a stream of abuse at each other, both on and off the field. There was further conflict when, just before half-time, another incident flared up between two brothers from opposite houses. The resulting fight ended with both of them being sent off, after the referee tried to force them apart and was set upon for his pains. When he tried to continue the match he discovered he had lost his whistle and a replacement had to be hurriedly found. The injured Robbidane had by this time returned to do battle, thus making the Robbidanes outnumber the Le Viviers. This was considered unfair and whilst the referee was running towards the home goal, the unfortunate man was hacked down from behind and his face pushed into a cow pat. Once again he was forced to leave the field.

Even with their superior number, and despite every determined effort, the Germans couldn't add to their solitary goal and the half-time whistle brought the memorable first half to its conclusion. Both teams trooped off the field, the Germans for a slice of orange, the St. Ouen's side for a glass of farm cider. Dozens of youngsters invaded the pitch for numerous make-shift games resembling something between football and rugby. The heads of both families gathered their sons around them for new instructions on how to play the Germans and beat the hell out of the rival family. Meanwhile the remainder of the spectators discussed the first half, arguing about their individual forecasts of the final outcome of the game. One thing was certain, none of the spectators left, enough had happened to ensure a captive audience for round two of the big match.

The Constable, who is the elected head of each parish, had intervened during the half-time period on behalf of the local side. After much fast talking the Germans had reluctantly agreed to substitutes for the players who had been sent off. After all, they wouldn't want it said they had only managed to win because the opposition was under strength. Therefore three new players were needed from somewhere amongst the spectators. This was the chance Clarrie had been waiting for. With so many females watching the match, he felt it would be in his best interests if he was out there playing a major role in the downfall of the German Army. He had always fancied himself as a centre forward being mobbed by the crowd after scoring a hat-trick. The Constable still needed to find two more players and, after searching until a few seconds before the kick off, finally agreed to take Clarrie. With a resolved shrug of his shoulders he said. "Come on Hedley, you'd better have a go as well. At least you should be better than no-one"

Now Hedley didn't share Clarrie's love of football. Sport had never interested him and the rules of the game were a little hazy. All he knew was that one side was supposed to get the ball into one net whilst stopping their opponents getting it in the other. Nothing to it, he thought, what could be simpler. He ran onto the pitch and, to fits of laughter, caught his gumboots on a mole hill, ending up in a heap at the feet of the referee. Hedley was sent out on the left wing where he would be out of harm's way, although this placed him close to the touchline where Mr. and Mrs. Ahier were standing.

"You'll be mucking out the cow stalls for the next month if you don't play well" called out Grandpa.

"And you'll feel the weight of my rolling pin if you don't score" chimed in Grandma.

They don't want much, thought Hedley. Play well and score a goal.

The whistle went for the start of the second half and Hedley rushed forward down the wing, colliding with Phillip Le Vivier who was coming up the field.

"You're going the wrong way stupid" shouted Phillip, picking himself up off the ground. "We changed ends at half time"

"Well I wish somebody would have told me" Hedley felt his shoulder where the collision had left a large red mark which would soon turn black. "First you kick one way, then the other. This really is a confusing game"

Phillip pushed Hedley out of his way and straight into the path of a German who was in full flight down the wing with the ball at his feet. They both ended up in a heap on the ground with the referee standing over them.

"One more foul like that and I'll have to send you off"

The poor man now had a matching bruise on the opposite shoulder and was even more confused than before.

"You idiot Hedley" screamed Grandpa. "Don't you know anything about football?"

"No I don't, and I don't think I want to"

He made for the touchline but Grandma raised her umbrella making him think twice about leaving the pitch.

"Play or there'll be no dinner for you tonight"

Hedley kicked a mole hill then wandered back onto the field of play. There was no way he wanted to miss his dinner even if it meant chasing the ball all over the pitch for the next forty minutes.

The second half was now in full swing with St. Ouen applying pressure on the German goal. Old man Robbidane was getting over excited as his sons surged forward for yet another attack.

"Kick it with your head Jack" he screamed at his youngest son, as a high cross came over. Everyone in his vicinity laughed until the old farmer retorted; "Well his brains are in his feet so maybe he'll kick better with his head"

The logic went over most spectators heads though no-one was about to pick an argument with old Ted Robbidane apart from Pierre Le Vivier. His voice carried across the pitch as he quipped; "He can't see to kick the ball, he's fallen over and is sitting on his eyes"

"Very funny" Ted Robbidane looked anything but amused. "At least he's facing the right way, which is more than can be said for your sons"

"Things are boiling up quite well" Grandpa whispered to his wife. "Another few remarks like that and we'll have wholesale slaughter on our hands"

"Shame they don't join forces and beat the Germans" Grandma, waving her brolly at Hedley who had fallen over another mole hill.

"I think that idiot keeps his eyes in the soles of his feet"

The Germans were eager for a second goal to clinch the game. They passed the ball swiftly up field towards their burly centre forward who aimed a fast low shot to the corner of the net. Somehow Claude Vibert managed to dive to his right and catch the ball. Amidst resounding applause he jumped to his feet and kicked the ball into the centre circle where Clarrie was waiting totally unmarked. He allowed the ball to pass over his head then rushed towards the German goal with the defence in hot pursuit. The goalkeeper came out to narrow the angle allowing Clarrie to lob the ball over his head into the empty net. The crowd went wild, especially the Ahier's. Grandpa grabbed his wife and planted a kiss firmly on her lips. Grandma yelled; "Well done Clarrie" whilst delivering her husband a swift blow across his back with her brolly. Even Claude Vibert came rushing out of goal to join in the celebrations.

He gathered his players around him."Listen lads. There's only five minutes to go. Let's drop the family feud until the final whistle and try to win this game"

The Le Viviers and Robbidanes looked at each other.

"We're all for St. Ouen Parish. Come on, let's show the Hun how to play football"

The next few minutes were fast and furious. Play went from one end to the other until even the ball felt giddy. Hedley just stood in the centre and watched everyone run passed him, first one way, then the other.

"Run, you idiot" yelled Grandma.

Hedley didn't know why he should run or where he was going. He charged up field as fast as his gumboots would allow. The German defence rushed back to cover him, giving Clarrie a clear run with the ball. He let loose a thunderbolt of a shot.

"Goal" shouted the crowd, as the ball sped towards the net.

"Aahhhh" shouted Hedley, as his speeding run brought his head in contact with the ball. Hedley fell to the ground and groaned. The crowd groaned. The German keeper grinned as he picked up the ball.

"Danker" he bowed to Hedley, then bounced the ball a few times whilst looking to find an unmarked player.

For days after Hedley tried to fathom out exactly what happened next. He remembered staggering to his feet just as the keeper kicked the ball out. The next second something hit him hard on the back of the head and a great shout went up from all around the field. Arms reached down and picked him up, hands slapped him on the back and everyone seemed jolly pleased with him. Looking around, his glazed eyes made out the sight of the German goalkeeper picking the ball out of the back of the net. He didn't appear to be smiling anymore. Grandma was waving her brolly at him.

"Oh God" he cried, and started running again.

The sound of a long hard whistle reached his ears and once again many hands slapped his back. Hedley tripped over a mole hill and lay on the ground totally exhausted. To hell with this football lark. He'd rather miss his dinner and muck out the cows than play anymore.

Without realizing it, he was the hero of the hour. He climbed to his feet and staggered towards the Ahier family.

Grandpa grabbed his hand and pumped it up and down. Grandma appeared pleased with him, although it was difficult to tell between her smile and glare. Clarrie promised him a bottle of beer and said he'd muck out the cow stalls for him the next day. The heads of both the Robbidane and Le Vivier families came to add their praise and Grandpa couldn't resist the opportunity to get in a dig.

"It takes the Ahier family to show everyone how to beat the Germans"

His chest swelled with pride, and with one arm around each of his footballers, he led his clan back home.

Hedley was still a little foggy as to what he'd done to deserve all the praise. He just wished Millie had been attending the match so as she could have seen him play. He felt certain she would have been impressed with him.

CHAPTER FIFTEEN

Black Butter

The summer of 1944 saw many changes in the fortunes of the German Army. After the D-Day landings, the allies had pushed through France and down the Cherbourg peninsula until, by the middle of June, gunfire could be heard fifteen miles from the east coast of Jersey coming from the direction of Barneville and Carteret. By the 16th of August the port of St. Malo had surrendered. The islands were now cut off from any source of supplies and the siege of the Channel Islands had started. The Germans were ordered to fight to the last man in defence of the only piece of British soil they had managed to capture during the terrible costly war. Stocks of most commodities were extremely low, causing conditions to rapidly deteriorate. The Germans did not hesitate in commandeering everything they could lay their hands on in the way of food, livestock and medical supplies. The farmers were required to grow as much food as possible to help feed, not only the local population of forty thousand, but also the German forces numbering approximately 16,000 and a further 1,500 foreign workers who had been brought over from the concentration camp on the northern Channel Island of Alderney. Even though the local people could see an end to the occupation, many feared that unless the end came quickly, a vast number of people would starve to death. The islanders feelings at this stage of the occupation were mixed, joy at the advance of the allied armies, and fear of the lack of food that accompanied the siege. Grandpa decided something had to be done to lift the moral of his small family. After giving much thought to the matter, the idea of reviving the traditional Jersey Black Butter Night came top of his list.

Black Butter had been made on Jersey farms for generations. There was only one other place in the world which had a similar event. Through the early emigrants from Jersey to America, who gave New Jersey its name, the traditional recipe found its way down to Pennsylvania where it is called Apple Butter. Sethee d'nier Beurre or

Black Butter Night is always accompanied by singing and dancing. In fact it is more of a festive occasion than a means of producing food. Although recipes vary from one parish to another, the basic ingredients are much the same. When the butter is made it is usually manufactured in vast quantities, with two or more farmers joining forces and pooling their ingredients and man-power. Grandpa used the most traditional of all the recipes and therefore required 20 gallons of rough, unfermented cider, 22cwt of sweet apples and 1cwt of Bramleys. The grated rind and juice of 22 lemons, 8 sticks of liquorice, 28lbs of white sugar, 1lb of cinnamon, ½lb of nutmeg and 1lb of mixed spices. To help provide the apples, Grandpa enlisted the aid of his cousin from St. Martin, Jack Le Chevalier. Jack had a large orchard on his farm and many farmhands to help with the picking, peeling and slicing. Over the phone Grandpa made all the arrangements and even though it meant moving all the apples from one side of the island to the other, it was decided to use High View as the venue because there were no neighbours in close proximity who would be disturbed by the party that would go on for 24 hours. Cousin Jack also agreed to provide the 20 gallons of rough cider as he had just made a new batch. Through Grandpa's connections in the black market the remainder of the ingredients were purchased, so all systems were go. The date for the party was fixed for the 29th of September. Everyone was looking forward to the party and Grandma was busy in her kitchen preparing for all the hungry mouths she would have to feed. Once again Grandpa had come to her aid with many of the items she was having trouble acquiring through the normal channels. She consulted her cook book, commandeered the services of Millie from all other farmwork, and proceeded to prepare for the feast.

"We must have some jam. The shop has run out so we had better make our own"

They sorted through the remaining food left in the larder but could find nothing suitable for making jam. Grandma scratched her head. Most of the items in the larder were needed for the Black Butter and mustn't be touched but Grandpa had over-estimated in some cases and there was plenty of lemons and bags of sugar. Grandma remembered something her mother used to make years before and sent Millie out to the barn to see how many carrots were left in the barrel.

"There's over half a barrel, and Grandpa said you can use what you want"

"Good. We'll make some D'la Gelee d'Carottes"

Millie had never seen carrot jam made before, so she watched with interest as Grandma washed, scraped and cut up the carrots, then cooked them until tender. The resulting pulp was put through a sieve and weighed, then placed into a pan with the sugar, 1lb of sugar to 1lb of carrots. Once the sugar was dissolved the mixture was brought to the boil until it became a thick paste. Grandma then allowed the jam to cool slightly before adding the grated rind of two lemons plus the strained lemon juice. She also put in a few almonds along with a drop of Grandpa's precious brandy. She did this whilst her husband was outside so he wouldn't see his favourite liquid being poured into carrot jam.

With the party night almost at hand Grandma baked an apple layer pie or Du Solyi. She only required pastry, sugar and apples for the pie and all these items she had in stock. Clarrie had been a big help. Under the noses of the Germans he had been out low water fishing. He knew just where to go and arrived back with a five foot conger eel.

"Off with its head and tail. I'll make some conger soup" cried Grandma. "With so many mouths to feed I'll have to use some of the body but we should have enough left over for a conger pie"

Conger soup had become a delicacy during the occupation and would go down well during the long night when the men were stirring the butter. As well as the conger meat, Grandma needed salt, a cabbage, 2 shallots, mixed herbs, borage and marigold leaves, parsley and thyme, plain flour, milk, the petals of a marigold, and some green peas.

"I'll go and find the marigolds" volunteered Millie. "I think there's some growing in the hedge"

Grandma was running out of pastry and decided to make conger cutlets instead of pie. There would just be enough for the men who would be doing most of the hard work. The main dish of the evening was to be a traditional Jersey bean crock.

"Ted Carre killed a pig yesterday so ask Clarrie if he'll go over and buy the trotters and a strip of back fat"

"How about some "Wonders" Grandma?"

"Of course. The party wouldn't be complete without Jersey wonders. Ask Clarrie to check the times of the tide"

"What on earth do you want to know that for?"

"Good grief Millie. I thought I'd taught you how to cook. Surely you know that you never make Jersey wonders when the tide is coming in. If you do the fat will froth up and ruin your cooking"

Millie shook her head. Old wives tales, she thought, but if Grandma believes it then better let her have her way.

"Come on girl, don't stand around. There's plenty of work to be done if we're going to be ready in time"

Grandpa was also kept busy. The old barn had to be cleared out and wood chopped to keep the fire going. There were tables and chairs to move and lights to fix up. Due to the blackout imposed by the Germans, all the windows had to be covered with sacks and a heavy tarpaulin draped over the door. No light would be able to escape but unfortunately neither would any of the smoke. Most would go up the chimney, but a certain amount would stay in the barn which couldn't be helped, so everyone would have to put up with it. Grandpa knew if they broke the blackout rule the Germans would halt the party and ruin the Black Butter.

At last everything was prepared. A large barrel of cider had been supplied to quench the thirst and Grandma made plenty of Du Chaude in case anyone felt the cold. This drink was a mixture of cider and milk with beaten eggs added. When drunk hot it sent a warm glow through the body on the coldest of nights. It was one of Grandma's well tried and tested drinks.

The families were starting to gather. All day the women had been busy peeling, coring and slicing the apples which were placed in turrines or earthenware jars. This was women's work and the men wouldn't lower themselves to help. Their part was yet to come and would last for many weary hours without a break. During the day the men were busy on the farm as the animals still had to be tendered regardless of Black Butter. Cousin Jack had brought along his accordion and Clarrie agreed to join him on the harmonica. It was going to be a great night. Sixteen people crammed into the barn with smoke everywhere, music blaring out, plenty to eat and drink and Jack Le Chevalier's farmhands for company. Amongst these were a brother and sister, Arthur and Velma Jegou. Their reputation had preceded them. Artie Arthur and voluptuous Velma were well known throughout the island. Clarrie rubbed his hands together in anticipation, whilst Millie gazed at Arthur's muscles. Yes, it was going to be a night to remember.

The fire was lit at seven thirty in the evening. Whilst the wood was catching well alight Grandpa greased the inside of the large brass bachin or basin with 2lb of lard. A trivet or tripod, was placed over the open fire and the bachin lifted on top. Jack Le Chevalier poured the 20 gallons of rough cider into the bachin and everyone retired for refreshments whilst the cider was reduced to half its measure. They had all gone into the kitchen for soup and coffee when Grandpa noticed Clarrie was missing.

"Last time I saw him was when we were putting the cider into the bachin" Jack told Grandpa.

Velma offered to go and look for him but Grandpa said he had to go into the stables anyway, so he would search for his grandson. It didn't take long to find Clarrie. He had fixed up a large length of pipe over the bachin leading out of the barn into the cold night, ending up in a bucket.

"What on earth are you doing?"

"If you catch the steam rising from the unfermented cider, allow it to pass through the pipes, then cool it down quickly, the liquid that will form should be Calvados"

The old man stared at his grandson. "You mean to tell me you are using an old style "Still" to make apple brandy?"

"That's right Grandpa" Clarrie looked pleased with himself.

"Well now I've heard everything. Move over and let me give you a hand. How much do you expect to make?"

"Only a few pints, but it will be worth it"

The two men watched the smoke come out of the bachin, rise into the pipe, out of the barn into the cold air and a slight but steady stream of clear liquid drip into the bucket.

"Good God boy, where did you learn to do this?"

"One of the farmers was talking about it last Saturday night in the pub. I didn't know if it would work but I thought it was worth a try"

"Come inside now before anyone else comes out and sees what we're doing. If we're caught then everyone will want a share and a few pints won't go far with this lot"

Inside the kitchen the party was warming up. There was just enough conger soup left for the two men to have a helping. It would take about two hours for the cider to boil to half its measure. Only then could the apples be added and the task of making the butter commence. Arthur was already setting his cap at Millie and Hedley was beginning to get jealous. How dare this young upstart come over from St. Martin and try to pinch his loved one from under his nose. Grandma could foresee trouble and decided to keep her rolling pin handy. This could turn into a busy evening for her as she had also noticed the looks Velma was giving Clarrie. Not if I can help it, she thought.

Clarrie had disappeared again. Grandpa was not worried this time because he knew just where the boy was. The two hours were up and the cider would be ready. All the pipes had to be removed and the traces of the illicit "Still" hidden away from the eyes of cousin Jack. After all, it was his cider. Clarrie re-entered to confirm that the cider was indeed ready for the next stage so everyone strolled out into the night air towards the barn. They were just about to start when Grandpa noticed something floating in the bachin.

"What's that you've put in the cider Jack?"

"A sprig of hawthorn. It helps to keep away any witches"

"Then what's Velma still doing here?" inquired Grandma, in a soft voice so as only her husband could hear.

"Will it keep the Germans away as well?" asked Millie.

Jack laughed. "I wouldn't know about that, but we can only hope"

The first 28lbs of apples were added to the cider and the "Rabot" which was the implement used for stirring the mixture was handed to Grandpa. As host, he had the honour of first stir. After the old man, every man present would take his turn at stirring the butter. A mark was made above the fireplace with a nail to keep tally of how many loads of apples went into the bachin. Grandpa had stirred Black Butter many times before and the younger men watched his fluent forward and backward movement across the bachin. If the stirring stopped for any reason or was performed in an incorrect manner then the butter would stick to the sides of the bachin and be ruined. Cousin Jack took out his accordion and the party got under way in the barn. Clarrie asked Velma to dance and Arthur grasped the opportunity to take Millie on the floor. Grandma's eyes never left them whilst they danced round and round the small barn. She knew as long as they stayed inside the barn Millie would be safe but if Artie Arthur tried to take Millie outside Grandma had her rolling pin tucked into her coat pocket. It was going to be a long night and she would have to stay awake or else rely on the two dogs to watch over her grand-daughter.

The nail made yet another mark on the wall above the fireplace. It was Clarrie's turn to stir the butter and he pushed the "Rabot" backwards and forwards across the bachin through the thickening mixture. The smoke was starting to make his eyes water. Coughing could be heard from the groups of ghostly figures who could be seen either swaying to the music or sitting around drinking cider. Bawdy jokes were being passed from group to group, whilst a few of the helpers, having made themselves comfortable on the floor and through intoxication, had passed peacefully into a deep sleep. Hedley had been getting more and more agitated as the hours went by. Arthur had hardly left Millie's side. At that moment he was whispering in her ear. Her giggles filtered back across the room to Hedley who clenched his fists in anger. This man had to be taught a lesson. The hardest part for Hedley to swallow was that Millie seemed to be enjoying his attentions. Grandma also noticed the happenings in the far corner. She had made no move yet but was keeping a watchful eye on the proceedings, ready for any move towards the exit of the barn.

"More apples" shouted Clarrie.

Hedley jumped up with a start. He grabbed another terrine of sliced apples and moved over to the fire, at the same time keeping one eye on Millie. Clarrie was busy stirring and expected Hedley to work around him. The two men collided just as Hedley was tipping the apples into the bachin and the turrine flew out of his grasp, landing on the floor and ending up in dozens of small fragments. Hedley opened his mouth to apologize but all that came out was his chewing gum - straight into the bachin. Clarrie stared as at least three sticks of well chewed gum slowly disappeared into the butter.

"You stupid idiot. Now look what you've done. There's definitely no chewing gum mentioned in the recipe"

Jack Le Chevalier roared with laughter. "Never mind Hedley my boy, it will go down well with all the cigarette ash Clarrie has been dropping in. Adds to the flavour you know"

Hedley picked up another jar of apples, successfully circumnavigated around Clarrie, and tipped them into the bachin.

Jack looked at the young man's red face and smiled. "Don't worry lad, Arthur's is all mouth and trousers"

"Let's hope for his sake he keeps them on" replied Clarrie, giving his grandmother a swift glance.

Tiredness had overcome many people. Bodies were laying everywhere and the music had long stopped. Grandma had developed a headache and, against her wishes, had been bundled inside the house and sent upstairs for a rest. Jack Le Chevalier was stirring the butter, Grandpa was having forty winks in the corner, Hedley was drowning his sorrows in farm cider, leaving Arthur and Millie together. Clarrie thought it was time to make his move. He winked at Velma and nodded towards the door. Only Jack saw them leave and he grinned at Clarrie, wishing he was thirty years younger and could be the one going outside with the voluptuous Velma.

"Where are you taking me?"

"I may not have any etchings but you can come and see my cows" Clarrie led the girl across the yard and into the stables. "Above here is a small loft where we keep the hay. We'll be warm and safe up there and no-one will disturb us"

"Oh Clarrie, you are so romantic" Velma climbed up the short ladder and disappeared into the loft closely followed by a smiling Clarrie.

Arthur had tried to induce Millie to leave the barn but to no avail. Not only was she scared of retribution from her grandmother but she had decided that Arthur was not for her. She didn't want to become just another scalp for him to brag about. She needed a man who wanted her for life, would care for her and be a father to her children. She could do without the kind of man who just wanted her for a night, didn't care if he never saw her again and most certainly didn't want to be a father to anyone's children. Arthur was becoming frustrated by Millie's constant refusals to his ardent but somewhat unromantic proposals. He was not her idea of a knight in shining armour and there was no way he would ever charm Grandma. After the latest point blank answer of "No" from Millie, the disappointed lover excused himself and went in search of the toilet. Hedley saw him go and slipped out of the door after him. The chance he had been waiting for all evening was at hand. Now he could challenge the intruder to fair combat and, with certain victory over the aggressor, restore himself to his rightful place as Millie's hero.

He found Arthur standing up against the cow sheds using the wall for a function it had not been strictly designed for. He drew himself up to his full height, gritted his remaining teeth, and strode purposefully over to the giant who was watering the weeds around the stable wall. The man who was treated as a subject of ridicule and hilarity had suddenly become a man of iron. A righter of wrongs and a guardian of damsels in distress. This was indeed a new Hedley. Though a few seconds later, as he picked himself up off the floor, he wished he had remained the old Hedley. His jaw ached and one more of his few precious teeth lay on the ground. What could possibly have gone wrong? Didn't the good guys always win in the stories he had heard or read about. The tall smiling giant, who should have been laying on the ground, was rubbing his grazed knuckles and grinning down at his vanquished foe. Hedley, his head still spinning from the blow it had received from those knuckles, just couldn't comprehend the reason for his present predicament.

Clarrie's present predicament was, on the other hand, much more satisfactory. Velma was living up to her reputation. There had been no refusals towards his advances. She had been only too willing to expose the beauty of her voluptuous body. He couldn't believe his luck. The couple lay on the hay, arms wrapped around one another. Velma's blouse, having been released from its duty, lay a few yards away and her bra had found its way down around her waist. Everything was going according to plan and Clarrie was preparing himself for the final assault. Unbeknown to the lovers, a small pair of evil eyes watched every movement. Whiskers twitched in the dark and four little feet ran across the loft passing over the outstretched leg of the lovely Velma. Her scream was enough to wake the dead of many generations. The rat, frightened by the sudden noise, ran back to his hole, once again passing over her leg. The repeat performance was too much for the scantily dressed girl to stand. She threw the startled romeo off of her body and rushed for the safety of the ladder. A little too much haste in her flight caused her downfall. The ladder was short but it was also unstable and care was needed when climbing or descending. Velma was too overwrought to take care in her descent and, with a further yell, shot through the opening, missed her footing on the ladder and landed in an unceremonious manner on top of a frightened cow. Picking herself up out of the mess which surrounded the poor animal, she proceeded on her ungainly exit from the cow-shed. Hedley's excuse for a brain was still a little foggy and the screaming hadn't helped. He was standing, open mouthed, outside the door of the stable when something white made a fast exit from the shed and, knocking him to the ground, ended up on top of him. This just wasn't his night.

The screams had brought everyone to life. Grandpa shook his head and rubbed the sleep out of his eyes. Cousin Jack smiled to himself. Clarrie my boy, he thought, you're in trouble. Bodies rushed out of the barn and came to a sudden halt at the sight that awaited them. Hedley was on his back in the mud with Velma laying on top of him, her left breast firmly pressed into his face. Grandpa stared at the apparition before him. Grandma came running out of the house with her rolling pin at the ready. Coming to a screeching halt by the side of her husband, she stared open mouthed at the spectacle. Velma pulled herself free of the struggling Hedley, covered her breasts with her hands, which was not an easy job, then disappeared into the kitchen. Grandma followed her, eager to question the young lady. Grandpa helped Hedley to his feet and led him towards the barn. Clarrie, who had come down in a slower manner from the loft, watched the goings on through the stable window. His silent laughter was a little premature because at that exact moment Grandma was hearing the full story from a sobbing Velma. Jack Le Chevalier smiled to himself as he stirred the butter. A day on his cousin's farm was always good for a few laughs.

Everyone appeared to have a second wind after this incident. Grandma knew the true story and she was going to wait until she could corner Clarrie when no-one else was around. Cousin Jack knew, Grandpa guessed, the remainder of the gathering thought Hedley had been up to no good. They couldn't understand how he had managed to get Velma into such a state. Usually she either allowed the man to have his way or kicked him somewhere that would stop any further monkey business dead in its tracks. Arthur seemed quiet about the whole affair. He hoped his knuckles would heal in time for him to give Clarrie the same treatment Hedley had received. There was no doubt in his mind who was responsible for his sister being in an undressed condition. Retribution would be dealt out at a later date when there were no witnesses. Hedley didn't know what to think. His little grey cells were throbbing from trying to work out just what had happened to him. Half the people there were treating him like a hero and slapping him on the back, calling him a good fellow. It must be said that most of these were men. The women huddled together in one corner and would have nothing further to do with the poor man. He hadn't done anything but challenge Arthur to a fight over Millie and had lost. How Velma came to be laying on top of him with her chest bare was a mystery. Hedley smelt a rat in the woodpile. A rat named Clarrie.

All the sweet apples had now been put into the mixture. It was time to add the Bramleys. An argument started between Grandpa and cousin Jack as to whether the sugar should be added now or left until the end.

"I have always put the sugar in before the Bramleys"

"Then you've always done it wrong" answered Jack. "The sugar goes in once you've taken the bachin off the fire"

"That won't give it time to dissolve and mix in properly with the apples"

So the argument continued. Grandma looked at the two men and shook her head. Just like two little boys, she thought. The old lady picked up a bag of sugar and poured it into the butter.

"Now I've settled the argument. Could we please carry on with the job in hand. Time is running out and dawn will soon be breaking" The rest of the sugar was added. Two men were now required to stir the butter as it had become quite thick. When half the Bramleys had been put into the butter the spices were added. The strong smell wafted around the barn causing a few people to sneeze. Then the lemons were squeezed and the juice poured into the bachin along with the grated rind. The butter was now taking on a dark brown colour and was of a fairly thick consistency. Grandpa took a sample out of the bachin and pronounced it ready. Using sacking as webbing, four men lifted the bachin off the trivet and onto the floor of the barn. A table had been prepared by the women on one side of the barn with a large collection of jars. Whilst the butter was still hot, buckets of the bubbling mixture was carried over to the table where the women began to fill the jars with the finished product. When each jar was full it had to be banged on the table to expel the air out of the butter. Then a piece of paper was placed over the top with an elastic band to hold it in place. It was a further two hours before the Bachin was finally empty and over 350 jars of Black Butter had been potted. The job of clearing up could be tackled by Hedley later in the day. Everyone was invited into the kitchen for coffee and only then did Velma put in an appearance. She had been in the house since the unfortunate incident and Grandma had sent Millie to keep her company. This was her way of stopping any further trouble.

"Good of you to help Jack" Grandpa shook hands with his cousin who was about to leave.

"Wouldn't have missed it for the world. Thank God I'm not really related to you though. It's hard enough being friends with someone who gets the recipe for Black Butter wrong"

Clarrie had overheard the conversation. "I thought you two were cousins"

"J'nos accousinons, car tous les Jerrias sont cousins"

Clarrie knew enough Jersey patois to understand his grandfather. After years of interbreeding the saying was probably true.

"We call each other cousins, for all Jersey people are cousins"

"Goodbye then cousin" Clarrie waved to Arthur. "Say goodbye to cousin Velma for me"

"Arbidot everyone" called out Jack. "See you again soon"

– 1944 –
CHAPTER SIXTEEN

Cousin Clara

For the past few days the same German soldier had been wandering around the vicinity of the farm. His aimless strolling up and down the road was beginning to get on everyone's nerves. Grandpa was getting jumpy, whilst Grandma virtually kept Millie a prisoner in the house. This German was after something. He never came too close to the farm and hadn't tried to enter into conversation with any of the occupants. Just when he seemed to have moved on and the family started to relax, his small frail figure appeared around the corner. He had a slight limp and stopped to rest every so often. He leant on the hedge with his elbows, allowing his small head to rest in his cupped hands. Bright little piggy eyes darted from side to side, taking in the layout of the farm and everything it had to offer. Grandpa called a meeting. There was no doubt in his mind. This German was only after one thing. Precautions must be taken to ensure that when he made his attempt it would be unsuccessful. The meeting would decide the best form of defence. No effort would be spared to stop the short lean soldier attaining his goal. The German was after food.

Food had been short for sometime. Everyone on the island was beginning to feel the pinch. Even the Germans were having trouble keeping up the appearance of a well fed, satisfied army. The farms just couldn't produce enough food to go round. The farmers had a plentiful stock in their larders and the farmhands were also well fed, but most of the other inhabitants were losing weight rapidly. Some German soldiers had even been seen helping themselves to the remains of meals that had been thrown out into dustbins. Potato peelings were on their menu and any stray dog or cat would be caught, killed and served up as a main course.

Various ideas were put forward at the meeting. Clarrie was in favour of giving the soldier a good hiding but Grandpa told him to use a little sense for once in his life, or be quiet if he couldn't come up with any reasonable, constructive ideas. The real problem was that the soldier hadn't done anything, even though everyone knew what was in his mind, there was no proof. Defence had to be the only way out of the situation. The dogs would be brought into the house at night whilst the barn would be made as secure as any old farm building could be. The stables which housed the cows, bull and horse, had a connecting door into the large barn in which the chickens and rabbits were kept. The goat had a special stall in the barn as the cows didn't like him at all and he didn't like anything or anybody. No-one on the farm was quite sure why Grandpa kept him. He served no useful purpose, only taking up space and eating grass that could have been used for the cows. Like the bull, Grandpa seemed to have a special relationship with the animal. He could be seen talking to the goat and stroking the animal whenever he was working out some new idea or other. Clarrie reckoned it was the goat who ran the farm, telling Grandpa what to do and how to go about it. He always joked that when his grandfather and the goat were crouched next to one another there was a definite resemblance.

Grandpa came up with the idea of bolting the doors and windows from the inside, thus making Hedley climb up the ladder from the barn into the loft and come out through the trap door used for passing down the hay, then down another ladder into the yard. This ladder would then be taken indoors at night so that the only methods of entering the barn would be either by breaking in, which would make a great deal of noise, or climbing up the outside of the barn and getting in through the trap door. The pigs were considered to be safe as they made enough noise when anyone entered their sty to wake up the dead. Besides which, Grandpa was certain the German was after the chickens. With these defensive measures approved by the family they set about making the barn and stable impregnable.

Once the windows and doors had been secured, Grandpa inspected the stables. Everything seemed satisfactory. The German would have to be extremely clever if he succeeded in breaking into the barn or outbuildings without disturbing anyone. The smell of Grandma's cooking brought the men into the kitchen for their mid-day meal. The window of the kitchen looked out onto the main road enabling a watch to be kept for the German soldier during the meal. Clarrie suggested his grandmother should go and sleep in the barn with her rolling pin at the ready. A swift backhander wiped the smile off his face. He was saved any further injury by the ringing of the phone. Grandpa left the table and answered the summons. The call went on for ages and he talked in a low voice so the remainder of the family couldn't hear what he was saying. Grandma was furious. She edged closer to her husband just as he replaced the telephone in its cradle. A smile covered his weatherbeaten face as he returned to the table. Grandma smelt trouble, Clarrie smelt the food on the range and hoped for a second helping, Millie smelt cow stalls, but then she was sitting next to Hedley so that wasn't unusual.

"Your cousin Clara has died" Grandpa looked at Clarrie. "Her last wish was to be buried in St. Ouen, so I want you to go over to Uncle Pierre's farm and collect her coffin. You can take the horse and trap and your grandmother had better go with you"

Clarrie had never heard of cousin Clara but no amount of pumping could produce any further information out of his grandfather.

"This will mean a great deal of extra work and preparation"

Clarrie didn't like the sound of all this extra work, especially for someone he didn't know. What was so mysterious about this cousin Clara anyway?

After dinner Hedley was sent outside to wash down the trap and brush the horse. The trap was covered with mud and it was an hour before it was fit to be used as a hearse. The horse took considerably longer. He didn't like the brush and gave Hedley much trouble before he was ready to take part in a funeral cortege. Petrol had become a luxury by this time so whenever possible, as in the case of farmers, coffins were carried by horse and trap. All Clarrie had to do was to pick up the coffin from his Uncle Pierre in the parish of Trinity and bring it back to High View where it would lie in state until Grandpa had made the necessary arrangements.

"You'd better wear some black clothes, and try not to stop at all the public houses you pass on the way back"

The old man seemed to have a twinkle in his eyes which Clarrie found off-putting.

"Your cousin Clara could never abide drink"

She sounded like a real live wire, thought Clarrie, as he went upstairs to get changed. Still it was a pleasant afternoon to go for a drive across the island instead of working in the fields. He hummed a little tune to himself as he hunted for his black tie. He hadn't had cause to wear it for over seven years and a thorough search of his drawers proved fruitless. Where on earth could he have put that damn tie? Grandma came to the foot of the stairs. "Hurry up Clarrie. It'll be dark before we're back if we don't get started soon"

Oh hell. Dark blue would have to do. Clarrie tied a quick rough knot in the blue tie hoping Grandma wouldn't notice the two grey stripes across the front. He threw on his jacket and slid down the banisters, narrowingly missing his grandmother, who had come to the foot of the stairs to give him one last call.

"Will you ever grow up? Just look at your collar" She proceeded to straighten his clothes.

"Leave it off Grandma. You make me feel like a little boy who still needs dressing"

"I know a big boy who is going to feel the weight of my hand in a minute. Where's your black tie? You look a mess to go and collect your cousin Clara"

"She won't notice" Clarrie instinctively ducked as his grandmother's hand flew towards his ear. "Come on Grandma. It'll be dark before we're back if we don't get started soon"

The drive to Trinity took almost an hour and Clarrie had a thirst for a large glass of farm cider by the time he had loaded the coffin containing cousin Clara onto the back of the trap. Uncle Pierre took them inside where their various needs were taken care of. Grandma settled for a cup of tea but Clarrie's requirements were well known amongst the family and Uncle Pierre placed a stone jar of cider in front of the young man and watched as Clarrie made short work of the golden liquid it contained.

"Look after Cousin Clara, she's been with us for a good few years now and we'd all grown fond of her. It's a pity but everyone has to go sometime"

Clarrie found the lack of tears or sombre looks amongst the family strange. Maybe she had been a right old battleaxe, he thought. They're probably glad to see the back of her if the truth is known.

Grandma glanced at the clock. "Time to be going"

"I know" Clarrie emptied his third glass of cider. "It'll be dark before we're back if we don't get started soon"

Grandma appeared nervous. She sat alongside of Clarrie with her sharp eyes darting from side to side. They crossed over the border of Trinity and slowly made their way through the parish of St. John.

"Don't get any ideas of stopping at the hotel" Grandma fixed a piercing glare at her grandson. "It's straight home my lad"

A troop of soldiers suddenly came round the corner. Grandma saw the men and immediately started crying. What on earth is going on thought Clarrie? The Germans made way for the horse and trap and, on a command from the officer in charge, took off their helmets as the coffin passed by.

Grandma wiped away the few tears from her eyes. "Take a short cut through the lanes"

Clarrie pulled on the reins and the horse begrudgingly turned left into the narrow lane. It was just wide enough for the trap and Clarrie hoped they wouldn't meet anything coming the other way or the short cut might prove useless. Sure enough, as they turned round a bend in the lane, another horse and cart was approaching from the other direction.

Both vehicles came to a halt. Centenier Blampied raised his cap to the old lady. "Good afternoon Mrs. Ahier. Not often we see you in these parts"

He noticed the coffin on the back of the trap. "Oh, I'm sorry to see you've had a bereavement in the family"

Grandma had started crying again. "It's our Cousin Clara. She was living on Pierre Ahier's farm in Trinity but wanted to be buried in St. Ouen"

The honorary policeman smiled. "I knew her well"

Clarrie picked up his ears. Here was someone who actually knew the mysterious Clara.

"Taking the back roads to keep out of the way of the Germans? We've had a great many funerals pass through here recently. There must be a sudden epidemic amongst the farmers of Trinity and St. Ouen. Was the death through natural causes or foul play? Maybe she slipped in the pigsty? Bury her deep Mrs. Ahier. Give Pierre my best wishes and tell him he must soon be running out of relatives. It's the third time in three months he's had a member of his family bury Cousin Clara."

Clarrie didn't understand a word of what was going on. This policeman didn't seem to be showing any respect for the dead. In fact he appeared to find the matter quite amusing. Clarrie was bewildered. How could Cousin Clara have been buried three times during the last few months? There was something fishy going on, and what ever it was had a strong connection with the contents of the coffin behind him in the trap. The policeman moved his cart to one side to enable Clarrie to squeeze through and proceed on his way.

"I hope the rest of your family stays healthy" he called out after them.

Dozens of questions were forming in Clarrie's brain, but one look at his grandmother told him to wait until he reached home when he felt sure all would be revealed.

The journey to High View seemed endless. Clarrie couldn't wait to get home and have all his questions answered. The horse appeared to sense his hurry and plodded along at a slower pace than usual. Grandma was not in a talkative mood. She sat alongside Clarrie staring straight ahead and her hands were shaking. Not with the cold, thought Clarrie. Something is definitely wrong. At last the roof of High View came into sight and even the horse put on a spurt. Grandpa was waiting in the farmyard and one look at his wife's face was enough to tell him that something had happened on the journey. Hedley was ordered to give Clarrie a hand into the stable with the coffin whilst the old couple went straight into the kitchen. Clarrie would have loved to open the coffin and have a look at Cousin Clara but having never seen a dead body he resisted the temptation. His thoughts were interrupted by the arrival of Grandpa into the barn.

"So you had a spot of bother along the way, did you?" The old man took a screwdriver from the shelf. "Well I guess it's time to let you have a look at Cousin Clara. Don't faint on me boy. She's not liable to be a pretty sight"

Grandpa unscrewed the lid off the coffin and placed it against the wall. Clarrie mustered up his courage and moved over to the open coffin.

"You might have told me Grandpa. If I'd been stopped and the coffin searched I would have been in real trouble"

"I know my boy, but I thought you would play your part better if you were unaware of the contents. Still, now you know, so give me a hand to lift her out"

During this conversation, Hedley had remained to one side of the barn. He didn't want anything to do with dead bodies.

"Come on Hedley. Give us a hand and you can have the two pennies from her eyes"

Hedley turned white. "Keep her away from me"

Grandpa smiled at the two men. "Alright, the joke is over. Hedley come over here. She won't bite you, you've seen a dead pig before"

Hedley moved over to the coffin. Inside, with a neat slit across her throat, was a large fat sow.

"It's the only way of transporting a fully grown unlicenced pig that we could think of. The Germans haven't discovered our trick yet and your Uncle has used this method a good few times. By the sounds of it though this could be the last occasion we will be able to bury Cousin Clara"

"We just have to hope the German who has been hanging around doesn't choose tonight to break in or we'll be in trouble" Clarrie pointed out to his grandfather.

"Don't worry, we'll carry Clara into the house when the coast is clear and Grandma can start cutting her up"

"What will happen to the coffin?"

"Oh we'll find some use for it. In fact I think I've got the gem of an idea. Clarrie cover the pig over and carry her into the house. I've got a little job to do that could kill two birds with one stone"

The women were busy cutting up Clara. Clarrie and Hedley were milking the cows whilst Grandpa pottered about in the barn. No-one was certain just what he was up to and he wasn't offering any clues about his new idea. The old man strolled out of the barn just in time to catch sight of the German soldier. Right on cue, he thought. Now to kill the first bird. He walked across to the chicken run. During the day they were allowed to have the freedom of the run whilst at night they were herded through a hole in the side of the barn and kept under lock and key. The old man looked around his collection of hens. He selected one that was getting old, caught it and, making sure the soldier was watching, rung the poor animals neck. He carried the bird out of the run and walked back to the barn.

"Clarrie, tell your grandmother we'll be having chicken for dinner tomorrow"

Clarrie stopped milking. What on earth was the old fool up to? They didn't need chicken with all that pork in the house. His grandfather's voice came across the yard again.

"I'm going to leave the chicken in the barn overnight and prepare it in the morning"

Grandpa was satisfied the German had heard and seen everything.

He went into the barn carrying the fowl and closed the door. Now for the second bird.

Grandma wasn't convinced. "What makes you think the German will rise to the bait? If he doesn't everyone will lose a night's sleep for nothing"

"I've whetted his appetite with the sight of the chicken. If he doesn't come tonight then he'll never come. You and Millie will be in bed anyway so you won't lose any sleep"

"If you think I'll get a wink of sleep with you all in the barn waiting for a soldier then you're mistaken"

Grandpa turned away from his wife and gave the two men their final instructions. Clarrie was looking forward to the night's work, as it promised to be slightly different from the hum-drum life on the farm. Hedley, on the other hand, thought the whole thing was dangerous and wasn't in favour of taking risks with the Germans.

Clarrie placed an arm on Hedley's shoulder. "Don't worry. What can possibly go wrong? There's three of us and only one of him"

"He might bring some friends and then where will we be? They might even have guns and shoot us"

"If they shoot you we'll send you back to Trinity in the coffin and ask Uncle Pierre to bury Cousin Hedley"

The old man settled the argument. "You're our trump card Hedley. Besides which, I say you're going to do it and that's final"

Hedley wasn't happy but stopped arguing. He knew which side his bread was buttered. Grandpa's word was law and anyone who didn't like it could find somewhere else to live. That is unless you happened to be Grandma.

"Right now, if we're all ready? Make sure you are not seen going into the barn and once you're in there don't make a sound"

The three men left the kitchen. With stealth, and by various routes, they made their way to the barn and slipped inside to take up their allotted positions. Now started the long wait. Clarrie wished he could have a smoke but Grandpa had been insistent, making him leave his cigarettes in the house. Even Hedley's chewing gum had been confiscated. They lay in the darkness with only the occasional movement of the cattle in the stable next door as company. This was going to be a long night.

The German had waited until after midnight. The anticipation of the chicken meal awaiting him in the barn made his mouth water. During the last few long hours he had sat on the hedge and stared at the farmhouse. He hadn't seen any movement since the family went to bed just after nine o'clock. They had made enough noise, in fact there appeared to have been an argument going on. After lights out everything had been silent. He had failed to see the three men as they made their way to the barn, but of course he hadn't been meant to. The soldier felt he had waited long enough. Now it would be safe to break into the barn and relieve these simple peasants of their chicken dinner. He climbed over the hedge and quietly made his way to the barn. To his surprise, he found the farmer had forgotten to lock the door. Normally warning bells would have sounded in his head when being faced with an unlocked door late at night, but the thought of the chicken had removed all caution from his approach. He opened the door and stepped into the darkness of the barn.

The beam of light from his torch picked out the features of the barn. He noticed the connecting door to the stables was open but the cows were all asleep. The chicken hung by its legs on the far side of the barn. It was his for the taking. He kept well away from the coffin, which had been placed in the middle of the barn on two large wooden crates, and made his way over to his prize. The knife cut through the cord that held the chickens legs and his hand grasped the bird. Suddenly the man froze. Something behind him had moved. He turned, allowing his torch to circle the barn. The light picked out the coffin in the middle of the room. A hand had risen from inside the coffin and was slowly followed by a head. The face was dead white and the body covered in a white cloth. Rising to a sitting position the corpse stared straight at the soldier.

"Boo" said the corpse.

"Aaaaarrhh" The soldier dropped the bird in fright.

Up in the loft Clarrie pulled the cord. The peg tied to the other end of the long string came out of its holder. The door was no longer held in place and slowly opened. Grandpa completed the planned exercise by kicking the sleeping creature hard in the backside. Now no goat likes being woken up suddenly in the middle of the night by a sharp kick in the rear. The billygoat shot into the air, found the door of his stall open and, straight ahead of him, the figure of a man. This must be the culprit who had delivered the kick. The goat charged. The corpse grinned. The soldier felt himself being lifted into the air by a tremendous force from behind. He crashed into the coffin, knocking it off the crates, and ended up sitting on the floor alongside the grinning corpse.

"Boo" said the corpse.

"Aaaarrrhh" cried the soldier.

The goat surveyed the scene and charged again. This time he had two victims to aim at. The men scattered. The corpse had suddenly sprouted legs and moved quickly out of the way of the charging goat. The German was not quite so fast. Once again he found himself lifted off the ground by the force of the goat's horns.

"Do be quiet" called out the corpse from on top of a large crate. "You're making enough noise to waken the dead"

Grandpa flicked the switch and the barn was flooded in light. The goat now had a clear sight of his target and chased the soldier round and round the coffin and crates. His screams brought Grandma and Millie running out of the house and over to the barn. The two women opened the door and had to jump clear as the soldier shot passed them closely followed by the goat.

"Is everyone alright?"

Grandpa's reassuring voice came from inside the barn. "Yes, we're okay"

Clarrie stood against the ladder with tears running down his face.

"Oh Grandma, I wish you could have seen it"

"Where's Hedley?"

A head popped up from behind a crate.

"Boo" said the head.

"Alright Hedley. The game is over. You were very good"

"Good" laughed Clarrie. "He was magnificent"

The noise had also attracted the attention of a passing German patrol who pulled into the farmyard. The officer in charge climbed out of the truck and looked at the unfortunate soldier sitting up in the trap with the goat waiting patiently at the bottom.

"Vat zee hell is going on?"

Grandpa came out of the barn and grabbed the goat by its collar.

"This soldier broke into my barn to steal one of my chickens. He must have allowed the goat to get loose and it chased him around the barn. The noise brought us out and we caught him red-handed"

The soldier was still shaking with fright. "Zee have a body in a coffin in zere zat has come to life"

"Nonsense" Grandpa turned to Clarrie. "Put the goat back and tidy up the barn"

The officer stared at the soldier. "So, you ver stealing zis man's chickens and ver interrupted by a dead body zat came to life?"

Grandma came out of the barn. "The body he is referring to is our Cousin Clara and she most certainly hasn't come back to life"

The old man stared at his wife. What was she playing at? The officer looked at Grandma standing in her night attire holding a large rolling pin in her left hand.

"I vill see for myself" He marched past Grandma and into the barn. The coffin stood in the middle of the room on two large crates. Inside lay the figure of a beautiful young girl, wrapped in white clothes, with two pennies on her eyes.

"So young and beautiful. Vat a vaste to have died at her age. My condolences madam. Zis soldier vill pay dearly for his night's vork"

He strode out of the barn and ordered his men back into the truck.

"Take zat soldier down to zee barracks. I vill deal viz him in zee morning"

Turning to the four people gathered in the farmyard he looked at each in turn. "It is strange zat only two of you are dressed in night attire and zee other two in vorking clothes?"

Clarrie looked at his grandfather who couldn't think of a good answer either.

Grandma came to their rescue. "They were playing cards in the kitchen. They often play till two in the morning. This other man is our farmworker and was in bed as you can see by his clothes"

The officer turned towards the truck. "Very vell. You vill not be disturbed by zis man again. I promise you of zat"

The unfortunate soldier stared out of the back of the truck and pointed at Hedley. "Zat is zee dead body"

"I have had enough of zis charade. Dead bodies don't valk"

"They don't talk either" replied Grandma. "Hedley, say something"

Hedley looked straight at the soldier and grinned.

"Boo"

– May 9th 1945 –

CHAPTER SEVENTEEN

Mother of the Free

Churchill's words were still ringing in his ears.

"And our dear Channel Islands are also to be freed today"

The broadcast had been made during the afternoon and there was still no sign of any British troops. The Germans were still in charge and that cursed bunker was still at the bottom of his field.

"I'll believe it when I see them marching up through town"

Grandpa had been his usual pessimistic self during the evening. Everyone else in the household was busy planning for the coming liberation and all he could think about was gathering vraic.

"There was a good high tide this evening" Clarrie pretended he didn't hear. "Plenty of vraic down L'Etacq for anyone who wants it"

Clarrie still didn't appear to be listening. He knew just what he was going to do in the morning. Down to the harbour and wait for the liberating forces. The vraic could wait for another day. Tomorrow was going to be a milestone in the history of Jersey and he wasn't going to miss it for the sake of a load of vraic. Grandma was busy baking a special celebration cake and the old man noticed the remainder of his brandy had found its way out of the cellar and onto the table.

"Bah; I can't get any sense out of any of you tonight. I'm going to bed"

The old man climbed the stairs. As he reached the top he stopped to gaze at the portrait of his brother who had served and died in the First World War. "We beat the bastards again" He cleaned the glass with his handkerchief and made for the bedroom. He was just as excited as the rest of the family but felt it could be a few days before anything happened. There had been stories the British had landed in Guernsey today, although the town people would say anything to pretend they knew something the country folk didn't. It wouldn't make sense the troops going to Guernsey first anyway. They could remain occupied for another five years without anyone knowing. No, they'd come to the main island first.

"I'll believe it when I see it" he murmured to himself as he pulled off his clothes and climbed into bed. The noise of the others downstairs having a party and his own restlessness made sleep difficult. The thought of being able to wander around his property without seeing German soldiers peering over every fence, and shops filled with all manner of good things they hadn't seen for years filled his mind. At last, after five long weary years it looked like they were going to be free again. "Thank God" he whispered as he finally drifted off to sleep.

It was a similar morning to the day five years ago when he had gazed across the water at the nearby coast of France and feared the coming of the Germans. Now he searched the horizon for the first sign of the British fleet. No smoke was visible. Nothing stirred, only the birds filled the air with their chirping as they busied themselves with their nests. They had remained free for the last five years. Life hadn't changed for them at all. The humans had suffered, the cows were thinner, food was hard to come by, Hedley had finally run out of chewing gum, Clarrie had drunk the last of the brandy during the night's party, but the birds had remained free to come and go at will. The old man wandered round the farmyard. No-one else was up yet. No wonder. Probably all had hangovers. Serves them right. He hitched the cart onto the horse and slowly made his way down to the beach.

It was indeed a beautiful morning. The sun glittered on the water and the seagulls were swooping low over the sands looking for any scrap of food they could find. A few Germans had come out of the bunker at the head of the small fishermen's harbour of L'Etacq and were drinking coffee. One came across and offered the old man a cup.

"It is over. At last I can return home to my studies"

The old man's blue eyes stared at the soldier. Not more than twenty years old. He could think of a few replies to give the German but somehow felt sorry for the lad.

"Thank you" was all he managed.

The coffee was hot and tasty and Grandpa allowed himself a few minutes break to enjoy the drink. It would take him all of an hour to fill the cart as it was backbreaking work. Clarrie usually did the job but today; well; the boy should be there when the troops landed. Something to tell his children about. He returned the cup to the soldier and started filling the cart with vraic.

An hour had passed and the cart was almost full. The young German returned with another cup of coffee, causing a further break in the work. Grandpa raised the cup to his lips causing his eyes to lift towards the sea. Something flashed in the sunlight. He shielded his eyes against the sun. The German had placed his rifle against the cart and was relieving himself by the wall. Across the rifle was slung a pair of binoculars. The old man picked them up and gazed out to sea. A tear slowly gathered in the corner of his eye and trickled down the weatherbeaten face. The sound of the thin crackling voice made the German turn quickly round.

"Land of Hope and Glory. Mother of the Free.

H.M.S. Beagle steamed slowly towards Corbiere unaware of the two men on the beach. Side by side they knelt praying. One thankful for liberation, the other thankful for an end to the war he never wanted to fight.

The words echoed over the silent bay. "This is my Land. Now I have Hope in the future. Glory be to God for allowing me to live to see the end of this infernal occupation.